Things I Love!	Things I Hate!
Making Lists	Mr. Belden (at the dragstore)
Mounds Bars	~~Boys~~
Writing Poems	Liver
My Room	~~Pumpkin Pie~~
My Wart	Mrs. Westvessel
Frank (my goldfish)	~~My Parents~~
~~Secret Bad Thoughts~~	Babies
Wedding Gowns	~~Boys~~
~~Washburn Cummings~~	~~Washburn Cummings~~
My Name	~~All My Friends~~
My Grandmother	~~My Name~~
My Friends	My Parents
Wordsworth	Hospital Rules
Christmas	
~~My Parents~~	
Memories	
Washburn Cummings (maybe!)	

Bantam Books by Lois Lowry

ANASTASIA KRUPNIK
A SUMMER TO DIE

ANASTASIA KRUPNIK

Lois Lowry

A BANTAM SKYLARK BOOK®
TORONTO • NEW YORK • LONDON • SYDNEY • AUCKLAND

RL 6, IL 008-012

ANASTASIA KRUPNIK
A Bantam Book / published by arrangement with
Houghton Mifflin Co.

PRINTING HISTORY
Houghton Mifflin edition published October 1979
3 printings through December 1980

Bantam edition / September 1981
2nd printing ... January 1982
3rd printing ... December 1982
4th printing ... September 1983

ISBN 0-553-15253-X

Published simultaneously in the United States and Canada

Bantam Books are published by Bantam Books, Inc. Its trademark, consisting of the words "Bantam Books" and the por-
trayal of a rooster, is Registered in U.S. Patent and Trademark
Office and in other countries. Marca Registrada. Bantam
Books, Inc., 666 Fifth Avenue, New York, New York 10103.

PRINTED IN THE UNITED STATES OF AMERICA

CW 13 12 11 10 9 8 7

For Kip

ANASTASIA
KRUPNIK

1

Anastasia Krupnik was ten. She had hair the color of Hubbard squash, fourteen freckles across her nose (and seven others in places that she preferred people not to know about), and glasses with large owl-eyed rims, which she had chosen herself at the optician's.

Once she had thought that she might like to be a professional ice skater. But after two years of trying, she still skated on the insides of her ankles.

Once she had thought that she might like to be a ballerina, but after a year of Saturday morning ballet lessons, she still couldn't get the fifth position exactly right.

Her parents said, very kindly, that perhaps she should choose a profession that didn't involve her feet. She thought that probably they were right, and she was still trying to think of one.

Anastasia had a small pink wart in the middle of her left thumb. She found her wart very pleasing. It had appeared quite by surprise, shortly after her tenth birthday, on a morning when nothing else interesting was happening, and it was the first wart she had ever had, or even seen.

"It's the loveliest color I've ever seen in a wart," her mother, who had seen others, said with admiration.

"Warts, you know," her father had told her, "have a kind of magic to them. They come and go without any reason at all, rather like elves."

Anastasia's father, Dr. Myron Krupnik, was a professor of literature and had read just about every book in the world, which may have been why he knew so much about warts. He had a beard the color of Hubbard squash, though not much hair on his head, and he wore glasses for astigmatism, as Anastasia did, although his were not quite as owly. He was also a poet. Sometimes he read his poems to Anastasia by candlelight, and let her take an occasional (very small) sip of his wine.

Katherine Krupnik, her mother, was a painter. Very often there was a smudge of purple on her cheek, or a daub of green on one wrist or elbow. Sometimes she smelled of turpentine, which painters use; sometimes she smelled of vanilla and brown sugar, which mothers use; and sometimes, not very often, she smelled of Je Reviens perfume.

In the bookcases of their apartment were four volumes of poetry which had been written by Myron Krupnik. The first one was called *Laughter Behind the Mask*, and on the back of the book was a photograph of Myron Krupnik, much younger, when he had a lot of hair, holding his glasses in one hand and half-smiling as if he knew a secret. Anastasia's father hated that book, or said that he did. Anastasia sometimes wondered why he kept it in the bookcase if he hated it so much. She thought it must be a little like the feeling she had had when she was eight, when she hated a boy named Michael McGuire so much that she walked past his house every day, just to stick out her tongue.

The second book of poetry by her father had a photograph of him with slightly less hair and a mustache; it was called *Mystery of Myth*. Her father liked it. But her mother didn't like it at all. The reason her mother didn't like it at all was because on one of the inside front pages it said, "For Annie." Anastasia didn't know who Annie was. She suspected that her mother did.

The third book was her mother's favorite, probably because *it* said, inside, "For Katherine." It was called *Come Morning, Come Night* and was filled with love poems that Anastasia found very embarrassing.

But the fourth book was her favorite. Her father's photograph showed him bald and bearded, the way she had always known him. The poems were soft sounding and quiet, when he read them to her. The book was called *Bittersweet*; and it said, inside, "To someone special: Anastasia."

Sometimes, when no one was in the room, Anastasia took *Bittersweet* down from the shelf, just to look at that page. Looking at it made her feel awed, unique, and proud.

Awed, *unique*, and *proud* were three words that she had written on page seven of her green notebook. She kept lists of her favorite words; she kept important private information; and she kept things that she thought might be the beginnings of poems, in her green notebook. No one had ever looked inside the green notebook except Anastasia.

On page one, the green notebook said, "My name is Anastasia Krupnik. This is the year that I am ten."

On page two, it said, "These are the most important things that happened the year that I was ten:"

So far, there were only two things on the list. One was, "I got a small pink wart." And the other was, "My teacher's name is Mrs. Westvessel."

Mrs. Westvessel wore stockings with seams up the back, and shoes that laced on the sides. Sometimes, while she sat at her desk, she unlaced her shoes when she thought no one was watching, and rubbed her feet against each other. Under the stockings, on the tops of her toes, were tiny round things like small doughnuts.

Anastasia described the toe doughnuts to her mother, and her mother nodded and explained that those were called corn pads.

Finally she wrote, *"Reason three:* Because I am dumb."

Not dumb in school. Anastasia, particularly after she had finally mastered the difference between minuends and subtrahends, was actually a very good student.

"I'm dumb," said Anastasia sadly to herself, "because sometimes — too many times — I don't feel the same way about things that everybody else feels.

"I was the only one at Jennifer MacCauley's birthday party," she remembered gloomily, "who thought green ice cream was nauseating. Everybody even *said* I was dumb, for that.

"I'm the only person in the world," she reminded herself, "— the whole entire world — who likes cold spinach sandwiches. That's really dumb.

"And now," she thought, "I'm the only kid in the fourth grade who doesn't like Mrs. Westvessel."

So reason *three* seemed to be the reason. "Because I'm dumb." She left it there, frowned, and closed her green notebook. "Sometimes," she thought, "maybe it isn't a good idea after all to make a list and find out the answer to a question."

But when Mrs. Westvessel announced one day in the fall that the class would begin writing poetry, Anastasia was the happiest she had ever been in school.

Somewhere, off in a place beyond her own thoughts, Anastasia could hear Mrs. Westvessel's voice. She was reading some poems to the class; she was talking about poetry and how it was made. But Anastasia wasn't really listening. She was listening instead to the words that were appearing in her own head, floating there and arranging themselves into groups, into lines, into poems.

There were so many poems being born in Anastasia's head that she ran all the way home from school to find a private place to write them down, the way her cat had once found a very private place — the pile of ironing in the pantry — in which to create kittens.

But she discovered that it wasn't easy. She hung the Do Not Disturb sign from the Parker House Hotel on the doorknob of her bedroom door. She thought that might make it easier.

She got herself a glass of orange juice with ice in it, to sip on while she worked. She thought that might make it easier.

She put on her Red Sox cap. She thought that might make it easier.

But it still wasn't easy at all. Sometimes the words she wrote down were the wrong words, and didn't say what she wanted them to say, didn't make the sounds that she wanted them to make. Soon her Snoopy wastebasket was filled with crumpled pages, crumpled beginnings of poems.

Her mother knocked on her bedroom door and called, "Anastasia? Are you all right?"

"Yes," she called back, taking her pencil eraser out of her mouth for a minute. "I'm writing a poem."

Her mother understood that, because very often

Anastasia's father would close the door to his study when he was writing a poem, and wouldn't come out even for dinner. "Okay, love," her mother said, the way she said it to Anastasia's father.

It took her eight evenings to write one poem. Even then, she was surprised when she realized that it was finished. She read it aloud, alone in her room, behind the Do Not Disturb sign from the Parker House Hotel; and then she read it aloud again, and smiled.

Then she read it aloud one more time, put it into the top drawer of her desk, took out her green notebook, and added to the list on page two under "These are the most important things that happened the year that I was ten," as item three: "I wrote a wonderful poem."

Then she flipped the Do Not Disturb sign on her doorknob to its opposite side, the side her mother didn't like. "Maid," said the opposite side, "please make up this room as soon as possible."

Her poem was finished just in time for Creativity Week.

Mrs. Westvessel was very, very fond of Weeks. In their class, already this year, they had had Be Kind to Animals Week, when the bulletin board had been filled with newspaper clippings about dogs who had found lost children in deep woods, cats that had traveled three hundred miles home after being left behind in strange cities, and a cow in New Hampshire that had been spray-painted red during hunting season so that she would not be mistaken for a deer.

During My Neighborhood Week, one entire class-room wall had been covered with paper on which they had made a mural: each child had drawn a building to create My Neighborhood. There were three Luigi's Pizzas; two movie theaters, both showing Superman; one Red Sox Stadium; a split-level house with a horse tied to a tree in the yard; two Aquariums; two Science Museums; one Airport control tower; three State Prisons; and a condemned apartment building with a large rat on the front steps. Mrs. Westvessel said that it was not what she had had in mind, and that next time she would give better instructions.

Creativity Week was the week that the fourth grade was to bring their poems to school. On Monday morning Mrs. Westvessel took them on a field trip to Longfellow's home on Brattle Street. On Tuesday afternoon, a lady poet — poetess, she should be called, according to Mrs. Westvessel; but the lady poet frowned and said she preferred poet, please — came to visit the class and read some of her poems. The lady poet wore dark glasses and had crimson finger-nails. Anastasia didn't think that Longfellow would have liked the lady poet at all, or her poems.

Wednesday was the day that the members of the class were to read their own poems, aloud.

Robert Giannini stood in front of the class and read:

> *I have a dog whose name is Spot.*
> *He likes to eat and drink a lot.*
> *When I put water in his dish,*
> *He laps it up just like a fish.*

Anastasia hated Robert Giannini's poem. Also, she thought it was a lie. Robert Giannini's dog was named Sputnik; everyone in the neighborhood knew that; and Sputnik had bitten two kids during the summer and if he bit one more person the police said the Gianninis would have to get rid of him.

But Mrs. Westvessel cried, "Wonderful!" She gave Robert Giannini an A and hung his poem on the wall. Anastasia imagined that Longfellow was eyeing it with distaste.

Traci Beckwith got up from her desk, straightened her tights carefully, and read:

> *In autumn when the trees are brown,*
> *I like to walk all through the town.*
> *I like to see the birds fly south.*
> *Some have worms, still, in their mouths.*

Traci Beckwith blushed, and said, "It doesn't rhyme exactly."

"Well," said Mrs. Westvessel, in a kind voice, "your next one will be better, I'm sure." She gave Traci Beckwith a B plus, and hung the poem on the wall next to Robert's.

Anastasia had begun to feel a little funny, as if she had ginger ale inside of her knees. But it was her turn. She stood up in front of the class and read her poem. Her voice was very small, because she was nervous.

> *hush   hush   the sea-soft night is aswim*
> *with wrinklesquirm creatures*
> *   listen (!)*

> to them   *move*   *smooth*   *in the moistly dark*
> *here in the*   *whisperwarm*   *wet*

That was Anastasia's poem.

"Read that again, please, Anastasia, in a bigger voice," said Mrs. Westvessel.

So Anastasia took a deep breath and read her poem again. She used the same kind of voice that her father did when he read poetry to her, drawing some of the words out as long as licorice sticks, and making some others thumpingly short.

The class laughed.

Mrs. Westvessel looked puzzled. "Let me see that, Anastasia," she said. Anastasia gave her the poem.

Mrs. Westvessel's ordinary, everyday face had about one hundred wrinkles in it. When she looked at Anastasia's poem, her forehead and nose folded up so that she had two hundred new wrinkles all of a sudden.

"Where are your capital letters, Anastasia?" asked Mrs. Westvessel.

Anastasia didn't say anything.

"Where is the rhyme?" asked Mrs. Westvessel. "It doesn't rhyme at *all*."

Anastasia didn't say anything.

"What kind of poem *is* this, Anastasia?" asked Mrs. Westvessel. "Can you explain it, please?"

Anastasia's voice had become very small again, the way voices do, sometimes. "It's a poem of sounds," she said. "It's about little things that live in tidepools, after dark, when they move around. It doesn't have sentences or capital letters because I wanted it to look on the page like small creatures moving in the dark."

"I don't know why it doesn't rhyme," she said, miserably. "It didn't seem important."

"Anastasia, weren't you *listening* in class when we talked about writing poems?"

Anastasia looked at the floor. "No," she whispered, finally.

Mrs. Westvessel frowned, and rubbed her jiggly bosom thoughtfully. "Well," she said, at last.

"Well. Anastasia, when we talked about poetry in this class we simply were not talking about worms and snails crawling on a piece of paper. I'm afraid I will have to give you an F."

An F. Anastasia had never had an F in her entire life. She kept looking at the floor. Someone had stepped on a red crayon once; the color was smeared into the wood forever.

"Iworkedveryhardonthatpoem," whispered Anastasia to the floor.

"Speak up, Anastasia."

Anastasia lifted her head and looked Mrs. Westvessel in the eye. "I worked very, very hard on that poem," she said, in a loud, clear voice.

Mrs. Westvessel looked terribly sad. "I can tell that you did, Anastasia," she said. "But the trouble is that you didn't listen to the instructions. I gave very, very careful instructions to the class about the kind of poems you were to write. And you were here that day; I remember that you were.

"Now if, in geography, I explained to the class just how to draw a map, and someone didn't listen, and drew his own kind of map" (everyone glanced at Robert Giannini, who blushed — he had drawn a beautiful map of Ireland, with cartoon figures of people throwing bombs all over it, and had gotten an F.) "even though it was a very *beautiful* map, I would have to give that person a failing grade because he didn't follow the instructions. So I'm afraid I will have to do the same in this case, Anastasia.

"I'm sorry," said Mrs. Westvessel.

"I just bet you are," thought Anastasia.

"If you work hard on another, perhaps it will be better. I'm *sure* it will be better," said Mrs. Westvessel. She wrote a large F on the page of poetry, gave it back to Anastasia, and called on the next student.

At home, that evening, Anastasia got her green notebook out of her desk drawer. Solemnly, under "These are the most important things that happened the year that I was ten," in item three, she crossed out the word *wonderful* and replaced it with the word *terrible*.

"I wrote a terrible poem," she read sadly. Her goldfish, Frank, came to the side of his bowl and moved his mouth. Anastasia read his lips and said, "Blurp blurp blurp to you too, Frank."

Then she turned the pages of her notebook until she came to a blank one, page fourteen, and printed carefully at the top of the right-hand side: THINGS I HATE.

She thought very hard because she wanted it to be an honest list.

Finally she wrote down: "Mr. Belden at the drugstore." Anastasia honestly hated Mr. Belden, because he called her "girlie," and because once, in front of a whole group of fifth grade boys who were buying baseball cards, he had said the rottenest, rudest thing she could imagine anyone saying ever, and especially in front of a whole group of fifth grade boys. Mr. Belden had said, "You want some Kover-up Kreme for those freckles, girlie?" And she had not been anywhere *near* the Kover-up Freckle Kreme, which was $1.39 and right between the Cuticura Soap and the Absorbine Jr.

Next, without any hesitation, Anastasia wrote down "Boys." She honestly hated boys. All of the fifth grade boys buying baseball cards that day had laughed.

"Liver" was also an honest thing. Everybody in the world hated liver except her parents.

And she wrote down "pumpkin pie," after some thought. She had *tried* to like pumpkin pie, but she honestly hated it.

And finally, Anastasia wrote, at the end of her THINGS I HATE list: "Mrs. Westvessel." That was the most honest thing of all.

Then, to even off the page, she made a list on the left-hand side: THINGS I LOVE. For some reason it was an easier list to make.

Her parents were having coffee in the living room. "They're going to find out about the F when they go for a parent-teacher conference," thought Anastasia. "So I might as well show them." She took her poem to the living room. She held it casually behind her back.

"You guys know," she said, "how sometimes maybe someone is a great musician or something — well, maybe he plays the trumpet or something really well — and then maybe he has a kid, and it turns out the kid isn't any good at *all* at playing the trumpet?" Her parents looked puzzled.

"No," said her father. "What on earth are you talking about?"

She tried again. "Well, suppose a guy is a terrific basketball player. Maybe he plays for the Celtics and he's almost seven feet tall. Then maybe he has a kid, a little boy, and maybe the little boy *wants* to be a great basketball player. But he only grows to be five feet tall. So he can't be any good at basketball, right?"

"Is it a riddle, Anastasia?" her mother asked. "It seems very complicated."

"What if a man is a really good poet and his daughter tries to write a poem — I mean tries *really hard* — and the only poem she writes is a *terrible* poem?"

"Oh," said her father. "Let's see the poem, Anastasia."

Anastasia handed the poem to her father.

He read it once to himself. Then he read it aloud. He read it the way Anastasia had tried to, in class, so that some of the words sounded long and shuddery.

When he came to the word "night" he said it in a voice as quiet as sleep. When he had finished, they were all silent for a moment. Her parents looked at each other.

"You know, Anastasia," her father said, finally. "Some people — actually, a *lot* of people — just don't understand poetry."

"It doesn't make them bad people," said her mother hastily.

"Just *dumb?*" suggested Anastasia. If she could change, under "Why don't I like Mrs. Westvessel?" the answer "Because I'm dumb" to "Because *she's* dumb," maybe it wouldn't be such a discouraging question and answer after all.

But her father disagreed. "Not dumb," he said. "Maybe they just haven't been educated to understand poetry."

He took his red pen from his pocket. "I myself," he said grandly, "have been *very* well educated to understand poetry." With his red pen he added some letters to the F, so that the word *Fabulous* appeared across the top of the page.

Anastasia decided that when she went back to her room she would get her green notebook out again, and change page two once more. "I wrote a fabulous poem," it would say. She smiled.

"Daddy, do you think maybe someday I could be a poet?" she asked.

"Don't know why not," he said. "If you work hard at it."

"How long does it take to make a whole book of poems?"

"Well, let's see. That last book of mine took me about nine months."

Anastasia groaned. "That's a long time. You could get a *baby* in nine months, for pete's sake."

Her parents both laughed. Then they looked at each other and laughed harder. Suddenly Anastasia had a very strange feeling that she knew why they were laughing. She had a very strange feeling that her list of THINGS I HATE was going to be getting even longer.

Things I Love!	Things I Hate!
Making Lists	Mr. Belden (at the dragstore)
Mounds Bars	Boys
Writing Poems	Liver
My Room	Pumpkin Pie
My Wart	Mrs. Westvessel
Frank (my goldfish)	

The rats. So they were going to have a baby.

Anastasia had been angry a lot of times.

She had been angry the day that she came down with the flu and had a temperature of 103° and had to miss the special Children's Concert that the Boston Symphony was doing, and her parents gave the tickets to the terrible Truesdales who lived in the upstairs apartment.

She had been angry at the paperhanger who insisted on wallpapering her bedroom with the wallpaper rightside up, when Anastasia preferred the way it looked upside down.

She had been very, very angry at the person who stole her new bike when she forgot to chain it to the fence outside of the J. Henry Bosler Elementary School.

But she had never in her life been as angry as she was the evening that her parents told her that they were going to have a baby.

"What are you trying to do, be in the *Guinness Book of World Records?*" she asked her mother. "You're too *old* to have a baby!"

"Thirty-five?" her mother asked, with raised eyebrows. "Thirty-five is too old? Thirty-five is going to put me in *The Guinness Book of World Records?* Come on, Anastasia. Thirty-five is the prime of life!"

"Ten is," muttered Anastasia. "Ten is the prime of life."

"Wrong, both of you," said Anastasia's father. "The prime of life is forty-five. *I'm* in the prime of life."

"Anyway," added Anastasia, "you don't need a baby. You have *me*."

"Dumb, dumb, *dumb*," she thought immediately. "I'm being dumb, again. I'm the only one in the whole world, for pete's sake — the whole world including even my parents — who thinks that I'm important enough to be the only kid in the family."

Her mother sat glumly, examining some burnt umber paint on the back of her hand. Her father rolled his eyes the way he did every time the Patriots missed a first down.

"Yes," he said. "We certainly do have you."

There was a long silence.

"So," said Anastasia, finally. "You're not going to change your minds?"

Her mother rubbed her middle softly with her paint-smeared hand. "It's too late for that, Anastasia."

"It's a *fait accompli*," said her father.

"You know I can't understand Greek, Daddy."

"French."

"Well, French, then. I can't understand French either. What's a *fait accompli*: another word for baby?"

"In this instance, I guess it is. A baby boy."

Anastasia hooted. "You guys may think I don't know anything, but I *do* know that you can't tell what kind of baby it is until it's born. What do you mean, a baby boy? Did you consult a fortune teller?"

"Actually," said her mother, brightening a little and pouring herself another cup of coffee, "it's really pretty interesting, Anastasia. They have this special test they do, on certain women. . . ."

"What do you mean, *certain women?*"

Her mother blushed. "On women who are thirty-five or older, if they're pregnant."

"See?" said Anastasia. "*See?*"

"And," her mother went on, ignoring her, "they did this test on me, and it showed that the baby is healthy. A healthy boy."

Anastasia kicked the rung of her chair with one sneaker. She was quiet, thinking. Her parents both stirred their coffee at the same time, and sipped, at the same time, as if they'd been rehearsing: one, two, three, stir, and one, two, three, sip.

"You have probably been thinking some about where you're going to put this, ah, baby boy, in this *extremely* small, extremely crowded apartment," Anastasia said.

"Yes," said her father with interest. "We have been thinking about that. Any ideas?"

"Simple," said Anastasia, standing up. "Very simple. It can have my room. Because I'm moving out. Excuse me. I have to go pack."

She stomped down the hall to her bedroom. In the darkest corner of her closet she found the heavy canvas bag that was left over from her father's days in the Navy; it had KRUPNIK M A stenciled on the side. Once, when she was smaller, her father had put her into it, pulled the drawstring closed, and carried her around the apartment while she giggled.

Anastasia took the orangutan poster from her wall, rolled it up, and put it into the canvas bag. Then she added three pairs of underpants and a box of crayons. Carefully she put in her green notebook and a sweat shirt with a picture of Amelia Earhart. Sadly, she realized that she couldn't pack her goldfish. But her comic books went in, and a box of Kleenex, and a folded program from a performance of *Peter Pan*. Reluctantly she added her arithmetic book. Then she cleaned her water-color brushes in the glass of muddy water that had been on her desk for a week, put the brushes into her box of paints, and tucked that into the bag. Under her bureau was a rather stale Hostess Twinkie. She added that.

Then she went back to the kitchen. Her parents were still drinking coffee, looking distressed, and talking to each other quietly.

"Excuse me for interrupting. But I would like to have my silver cup, the one with my name on it, that my grandmother gave me when I was born. You don't have to polish it or anything."

Her mother went to the cupboard to look for the cup.

"You know, Anastasia," said her father. "The baby won't be born until March. So there's no need to hurry in making a decision about moving out. I would think that you'd like to stay through Christmas at least."

Anastasia didn't say anything. But she began to think. It would be nice to be around for Christmas.

Her mother was holding the little blackened cup.

"I really should polish this," she said. "You can barely see the name."

"That's *another* thing," said Anastasia. "What are you going to *name* this baby?"

"Goodness," said her mother. "We haven't even thought about that. Maybe you have some suggestions . . ."

"As a matter of fact," said her father, "I think we should give Anastasia the full responsibility for naming the baby. It will be her brother, after all."

"Of course, I won't be here," said Anastasia.

"That's right," said her father. "I forgot that for a minute. Tell you what, though. If by some chance you should decide to stick around, you may name the baby."

"Anything I want?"

"Well," said her mother, "maybe we should . . ."

"Anything you want," said her father decisively.

Anastasia stood there, thinking.

"Okay," she said, finally. "I'll stick around, and I'll name the baby. You can put the cup back."

She returned to her room and unpacked. Twinkie, paints, arithmetic book, *Peter Pan* program, Kleenex, sweat shirt, green notebook, crayons, underpants, and orangutan. She put the KRUPNIK M A canvas bag back on the floor of her closet. She had been thinking the entire time she was unpacking.

Then she sat down on her bed, picked up a pencil from the floor, and opened the green notebook to one of the very last pages where nothing was written at all.

In a secret corner, very small, she wrote the name she had chosen for her parents' baby boy. It was the most terrible name she could think of. When she had written it, she smiled and closed the notebook.

Things I Love!	Things I Hate!
Making Lists	Mr. Belden (at the drugstore)
Mounds Bars	Boys
Writing Poems	Liver
My Room	Pumpkin Pie
My Wart	Mrs. Westvessel
Frank (my goldfish)	My Parents
	Babies

"Reasons for maybe becoming a Catholic," wrote Anastasia in her green notebook.

1. There are fourteen Catholics in the fourth grade, and four Jews, and everybody else is something else — I don't know what — but whatever it is is not very interesting. So I would make the fifteenth Catholic. And if ever they start a club or something, I would automatically be in it. That would be nice.

2. And I would get a new name. Maybe at about the same time I get a new brother.

Anastasia thought vaguely that probably there were other good reasons for becoming a Catholic. But she didn't know what the other reasons might be; and the ones she had listed seemed good enough.

"I think I might become a Catholic," she said to Jennifer MacCauley, who she hoped was going to be her very best friend in the fourth grade. Jennifer had a lot of things going for her: she had naturally curly reddish-brown hair, a broken-off front tooth from falling down the basement stairs, and more Barbie doll clothes than any other girl in the class.

She also, she had told Anastasia, was before long going to have a new and very impressive name. Right now her name was Jennifer Elizabeth MacCauley. But one of these days, she said, she was changing her name to Jennifer Elizabeth Theresa MacCauley. That was because she was Catholic.

Catholics, Jennifer told Anastasia, were allowed to give themselves an extra name when they were old enough. They were even allowed to choose the name themselves; Jennifer had already chosen Theresa.

That appealed to Anastasia, who had never liked her own name very much, and who had no middle name at all. When her brother was born, she knew, *his* new name was going to cause — well, maybe not trouble, but talk. It was certainly going to cause talk. It would be kind of nice to get a new name herself at the same time.

"It has to be a saint's name," Jennifer pointed out.

Anastasia wasn't exactly sure what a saint was. But their names seemed okay. Some even seemed spectacular, for pete's sake. She looked at the list that Jennifer showed her.

"Perpetua," she said, reading from the list. "Anastasia Perpetua Krupnik. I like that. I definitely think I might become a Catholic."

"You can't," said Jennifer apologetically. "You're too old."

"What do you mean, too old?" asked Anastasia. "I'm only ten."

"Look," said Jennifer. She opened the top drawer of her desk — they were in Jennifer's bedroom — and searched through the broken crayons, crumpled spelling papers, and half a deck of cards. She found a snapshot and handed it to Anastasia.

"Big deal," Anastasia said, looking at it. "That's just you in a bride's outfit." Secretly, she looked a little harder and was envious. She had wondered, often, what it would feel like to wear a bridal gown. Not that she ever wanted to get married. Or to have a *baby*, for pete's sake.

"Ha," said Jennifer. "Bride's outfit, my foot. That's my First Holy Communion dress. I was seven. Everyone is around seven when they make their First Holy Communion. After that you're a real Catholic."

"Liar," said Anastasia.

"No, honest," Jennifer said. "Really. You can't be a Catholic unless you do that."

"Is there a law that you have to be seven?"

"I guess so."

Anastasia thought it over carefully. "There can't be," she said, finally. "What if you were on a trip around the world the whole time you were seven?"

Jennifer shrugged. "I don't know," she admitted.

"What if you had leprosy when you were seven?"

Jennifer looked confused.

"What if you were *Jewish* when you were seven?"

Finally Jennifer said, "Well, sometimes there's something they do in the Catholic Church. They give a disp — , they give a dispen — , a dispensation. That's what they give."

"What's that?"

"It means that you can do something against the Catholic rules."

"So. I'll get a dispensation, then. What do I have to do?"

"I don't know. You have to go to the church, I guess, and talk to the priest."

"Couldn't you do it, Jennifer? Couldn't you talk to the priest and bring my dispensation home for me? Like picking up the homework assignment from Mrs. Westvessel if I'm absent?"

"I don't know, Anastasia."

"For a Catholic, you sure don't know much, Jennifer."

Jennifer looked uncomfortable.

Anastasia sighed. "When do you go to church next?" she asked.

"Saturday."

"I'll come with you then, on Saturday. I'll talk to them about getting the dispensation. Probably I can bring it home with me. Then how long will it take to be a Catholic?"

"A while. You'll have to go to catechism classes."

"Well, that's okay. I want my mother to have time to order new nametapes for my camp clothes, since my name will be different."

"You don't have to put your whole name on things. I don't have my whole name on my camp clothes."

"Listen, Jennifer, do you think I'm going to become a Catholic and get a name like Anastasia Perpetua Krupnik and not let people *know* about it?"

Anastasia went home. She wanted to tell her parents about her decision to become a Catholic, but she knew that she had to tell them at the right moment, in the right way, because it would be something of a surprise. They might even be a little upset, she suspected, that she was changing her name.

So she waited until they were seated at the kitchen table for supper, waited until her mother had served the stewed chicken, and then she stood up and said, "Look." She began to sign herself with the sign of the cross, the way Jennifer MacCauley had showed her. She got mixed up and realized she was doing it backwards.

"Wait a minute," she said. Then she said aloud, thinking, "Forehead. Belly button. Left nipple. Right nipple." She did it again, correctly.

Her parents looked at her, puzzled.

"That's terrific, Anastasia," her father said, finally. "Look at mine." He stood up and said, "Nose. Stomach. Left ear. Right ear." He touched them in that order and sat back down. Her mother shook her head as if she thought they were both crazy.

"*Daddy*," said Anastasia angrily, "don't make fun of me. I was doing the sign of the cross. I'm going to become a Catholic."

"You're *what?*" said her mother.

"That is both interesting and preposterous," said her father, and began eating his chicken.

"I am too," said Anastasia. "First, I'm going to the church on Saturday with Jennifer, and talk to the guy there about picking up my dispensation."

"Oh?" said her mother, with interest.

"And then I'm going to catechism classes. I'm not sure how many I have to go to."

"Oh?" said her father.

"And then I have to get a wedding dress, and then I make my First Holy Communion."

"A wedding dress?" asked her mother.

"Yes. They make them in small sizes for Catholics."

"And then?"

"Well, you may not like this part much. But then I change my name. I will be Anastasia Perpetua Krupnik."

Her parents looked at each other thoughtfully, and then they both looked at Anastasia.

"And that's it?" asked her father.

"Yes. Then I'm a Catholic."

"You know," said Anastasia's mother, "most people, making an important decision like that, would discuss it first with their parents."

Anastasia looked pointedly at her mother's middle, which was beginning to bulge slightly so that she had left the button at the top of her jeans undone. "Most people," she said to her mother, "making an important decision like *that* would discuss it first with their child."

They each took a bite of chicken. Finally Anastasia's father said, "You're going to church Saturday, you said? To pick something up?"

"Yes, my dispensation. I'll show it to you when I get home."

"Fine. I suggest that we don't really need to discuss this any more now. We'll wait till Anastasia has been to the church and talked to the, ah, the guy there, about everything."

They all nodded. Anastasia's mother passed the peas around again, and they began to talk about names, in general. Dr. Krupnik said that the funniest name he knew of was that of a new Harvard instructor in Economics: Weatherly Scarf.

Mrs. Krupnik said that Weatherly Scarf wasn't as funny as the name of a model who had once posed for Life classes when she was an art student. The model had been named Felicity Brest.

Anastasia thought that neither of those names was as funny as the name that she was going to name their new baby in March. But she didn't say that.

And no one said anything at all about the name Anastasia Perpetua Krupnik.

It was raining on Saturday, but Anastasia wore her best dress anyway, underneath her yellow slicker, and carried a large Lord and Taylor's shopping bag, just in case she needed it for carrying the dispensation home.

She and Jennifer MacCauley walked along Brattle Street toward St. Cecilia's Catholic Church.

"I never knew before that Catholics went to church on Saturday," Anastasia said. "I thought only Jewish people did that."

"Oh," said Jennifer, "we're not really going to church today. We go to church tomorrow, on Sunday. But on Saturday we go to confession. That's where we're going now, to confession."

Anastasia looked at Jennifer and giggled. *"Confession?* That's just for criminals, like when they're in the police station and the cops talk to them for a long time, and maybe beat them up a little; then they finally confess."

"Well, this is sort of the same thing, only there's no police or anything, and they don't put you in jail. You just go to the church and confess your sins."

"I won't have to do that part. Because I don't have any sins."

"You do, too. Everybody does. They don't have to be *big* sins, like murdering anybody."

"I don't have any little sins, either."

"Liar. You told me you stole Mary Ellen Bailey's cupcake out of her lunchbox last week."

"A cupcake? That's a *sin?*"

"Yeah."

"If I'm a Catholic I have to confess about a cup-cake?"

Jennifer nodded. "And also if you think bad thoughts about anyone."

Anastasia stood very still for a moment on Brattle Street. "What if in bed at night I wish that Mrs. Westvessel would get a disease that would make pimples grow all over her face?"

Jennifer thought about that. "Yes," she stated, finally. "That would be a sin, to wish that."

"So I'd have to confess it?"

Jennifer nodded. They had started to walk again, and had almost reached St. Cecilia's Church. It took up the entire next block, and had stained glass windows of people looking terribly sad, some of them with arrows sticking out of their stomachs.

"And," said Jennifer, "you would have to say that you were sorry."

"*Sorry?*"

Jennifer nodded primly. "Most heartily sorry," she said.

"Even if I'm *not?*"

Jennifer looked a little embarrassed. "Well," she said, "if you're a good Catholic, you really will be sorry."

Anastasia stopped where she was, on the sidewalk near the corner. She looked at her Lord and Taylor's shopping bag.

"Jennifer," she said, "my bag has a rip in the bottom. I don't think it'll hold the dispensation well."

Jennifer looked into the bag, at the small rip in the bottom. "Yeah," she said doubtfully.

"So I think I'll go on home."

"Yeah," said Jennifer. "I understand."

"Mom?" called Anastasia, when she let herself into the apartment.

Her mother was in the room where she painted, standing in front of the easel with a long smear of pale yellow paint across the front of her shirt, right where the baby was beginning to make a small mound.

"Mmmmm?" answered her mother.

"Have you bought my wedding dress yet?"

"Nope. Not yet." Mrs. Krupnik looked at her canvas carefully, and changed a tiny stroke of yellow with a narrow brush.

"Well, forget it," said Anastasia. "I've changed my mind."

Things I Love!

Making Lists
Mounds Bars
Writing Poems
My Room
My Wart
Frank (my goldfish)
Secret Bad Thoughts
Wedding Gowns

Things I Hate!

Mr. Belden (at the drugstore)
Boys
Liver
Pumpkin Pie
Mrs. Westvessel
My Parents
Babies

"I have fallen in love," Anastasia told her parents one morning at breakfast. It made her feel a little shy to talk about it. But she felt that her parents ought to know.

Her father blew a ripple into his coffee thoughtfully. "You seem a little young for that," he said.

"No, Myron," said Anastasia's mother. "She isn't too young at all. I myself fell in love for the first time when I was ten." She blushed a little.

"You *did*? With whom?" Anastasia's father always knew the right time to say whom. Anastasia had not yet mastered that.

"His name was Edward Mark." She blushed a little more.

"Edward Mark what?" asked Anastasia's father. Both of them seemed to have forgotten Anastasia altogether.

"That was all. Mark was his last name."

"Well, that's ridiculous. How on earth could you have gotten involved with someone who had two first names?"

"Myron, I was not, as you so crudely put it, 'involved.' I was simply in love. It was Platonic. Edward Mark and I played Monopoly together."

That interested Anastasia. She happened to know that her mother was not a very good Monopoly player. "Did Edward Mark get into building hotels?" she asked.

"If you were going to get involved with a hotel magnate," said Anastasia's father, "why didn't you make it Conrad Hilton?"

"I'm not going to talk about it anymore," said Mrs. Krupnik primly. "This is an unproductive conversation." She began clearing the table.

Myron Krupnik sipped his coffee and looked at his watch.

"Well," said Anastasia finally, "wouldn't you like to know whom it is that I'm in love with?"

"Who," said her father. "Use the nominative in that instance."

"Who it is," Anastasia corrected herself. "Who it is, is Washburn Cummings."

"How on earth could you have gotten involved with

someone who has two last names?" asked her mother grouchily. But she was talking to Anastasia's father.

"Will you people please listen to me for a change? I am in love with Washburn Cummings. That's important. Washburn Cummings is in the sixth grade. Washburn Cummings is black. Is it going to bother you guys if I get involved with someone who is black? And who is older than me?"

"Older than I," corrected her father automatically.

"Older than I."

Anastasia's mother was standing by the sink. She very often made speeches while standing by the sink. "I don't care if you get involved with someone who is black, or in the sixth grade. I just don't want you to get involved with someone who is insensitive, or who is wont to trespass on the inviolate memories of childhood in a way that is completely lacking in charity or compassion."

"I don't know what you're talking about," said Anastasia. "Washburn Cummings doesn't trespass on anything as far as I know. Once he got kicked out of the movies, though, for being loud and obnoxious."

Neither of her parents said anything. They were glaring at each other.

"Well, listen, you guys," said Anastasia. "Maybe we could talk about it later. I have to go to school now."

She went to get her jacket. As she buttoned it up, she went back to the doorway of the kitchen. "Washburn Cummings," she said, "is the same height as me. I mean, as I. But his hair is about two feet higher than that. So altogether, counting his hair, he is about as tall as you, Daddy."

"That's interesting," said her father, who hadn't really been listening.

"Edward Mark," said her mother loudly, measuring out the words very carefully, "had the most beautiful head of golden curls I have ever seen in my life."

"Well, that's just terrific," said Myron Krupnik, rubbing his hand over his own head which had not had very much hair for a very long time. "I hope he's had a wonderful career modelling for Breck shampoo."

Anastasia walked to school, not at all certain that her parents had grasped the significance of being in love for the first time.

Washburn Cummings, in all honesty, did not even know that Anastasia existed.

But everyone at the J. Henry Bosler Elementary School knew about Washburn Cummings. On the day that he came to school wearing a tee shirt with an obscene saying printing across the front, and was sent home by the principal to change, Washburn Cummings made a quick trip around the J. Henry Bosler Elementary School, appearing briefly at the door of each classroom and opening his jacket to flash the tee shirt at the class. By the time that the principal heard he was doing it, Washburn Cummings had flashed every classroom down through the second grade and was already heading down the front steps, bouncing an imaginary basketball and wiggling his hips.

"Who was *that?*" asked Mrs. Westvessel with a puzzled look on her face, after Washburn Cummings had appeared in the door.

"That was Washburn Cummings," said the whole class.

"And what was written on his shirt?" she asked.

No one answered. A few people giggled.

"Who are my speed readers here?" asked Mrs. Westvessel. "Mary Ellen Bailey? Robert Giannini? Someone *must* have been able to read that tee shirt."

Mary Ellen Bailey blushed. Robert Giannini, who always carried a briefcase to school, went up to Mrs. Westvessel's desk and whispered into her ear.

Mrs. Westvessel blushed. "Well," she said. "Well. My *goodness*. Let's take out our arithmetic books, class."

On the way home from school, walking with Jennifer MacCauley, Anastasia wiggled her hips and bounced an invisible basketball.

"*Anastasia,*" said Jennifer. "That's disgusting."

"No, it isn't. It's just a thing you do to be cool. Anyway, I'll tell you a secret. I'm in love with Washburn Cummings."

Jennifer groaned. "How do you know? How can you *tell* when you're in love?"

That was something that Anastasia had thought about a great deal. She had stood in the corner drugstore, reading a questionnaire called "Is it really love?" in *Cosmopolitan* until the pharmacist, Mr. Belden, had said, "Pay for it or close it up, girlie." Short of money, overdrawn on her allowance, she had had to close it up; but she remembered some of the questions.

"You think about him all the time. You stop wanting to see other men. You . . ."

"You never see any other men anyway," Jennifer interrupted.

"Quiet. He appears in your dreams, usually as a hero. You . . ."

Jennifer interrupted again. "Washburn Cummings appears in your dreams? As a hero?"

"Yeah. I dreamed the other night that I was lost. I was walking on Huron Avenue, and I couldn't find my house anywhere. Then Washburn Cummings appeared, coming out from behind a tree, and offered to show me the way home."

"Ha. Was he wiggling his rear?"

"No. He was being very kind. And he was wearing a cowboy hat."

"Washburn Cummings's hair wouldn't *fit* under a cowboy hat."

"Well, in my dream it did. Maybe he'd had a haircut. Let me finish about being in love. You find yourself wanting to fulfill his fantasies . . ."

"What are fantasies?"

"Imaginations."

"Oh, great. What are Washburn Cummings's imaginations, do you think?"

"Well, one time I saw him on the playground with a transistor radio, and he was just sitting there listening, with a happy look on his face."

"To what? A Red Sox game?"

"No. It was Roberta Flack. I figure maybe he really likes Roberta Flack. I find myself wanting to fulfill his fantasy about Roberta Flack. I'm practicing singing."

"You can't sing. You didn't even make Glee Club."

"Only because she put me in the alto section, and in 'This Land Is My Land' we had to sing a different tune from the rest of you. I can't do that. But I can sing a tune okay. Listen."

They stopped on the corner, and softly, in her Roberta Flack voice, Anastasia sang, " 'The first time ever I kissed your lips . . .' "

Jennifer made a face. "The singing's all right. But the thought of kissing Washburn Cummings is absolutely revolting."

"That's because you're not in love with him. You wait, Jennifer. When you're in love with someone, everything will seem different. You'll *want* to kiss someone."

"Not someone who acts as revolting as Washburn Cummings," said Jennifer, and turned to go up her street. Anastasia bounced her invisible basketball all the way home, wondering how she could make Washburn Cummings notice her. Maybe Je Reviens perfume.

Hair. That's what would do it, Anastasia decided. Obviously Washburn Cummings was interested in hair styles. He kept a comb tucked into his own hairdo all the time; on the playground, sometimes, she could see him take the comb out of its perch and rake it upward through his hair.

"I'm going to take a shower and wash my hair before I go to bed," she called to her mother at 8:30 that night.

She used all of the shampoo, squeezing the last bright green globs from the bottom of the tube. Then she combed her wet hair flat, down to the tops of her shoulders, looked at it in the mirror, wished that there were *more* of it, and braided it into as many skinny pigtails as she could. Fourteen soggy braids. When she went to bed it was like sleeping with her head on a complicated pile of twisted rope.

But it worked. In the morning she unbraided all the pigtails, combed it up instead of down, and looked into the mirror in amazement. It was as much like Washburn Cummings's hair as shoulder-length bright yellow hair could possibly be. She squashed it into her blue knitted ski cap before she went in for breakfast.

"One might ask," said her mother, "why you are wearing a ski hat to breakfast in November."

"One might ask that," said Anastasia, with her mouth full.

"One might also ask," said her father, "why I am wearing socks that don't match." He held up his feet, carefully keeping his balance on the kitchen chair. One sock was dark blue; the other was dark brown. "It's because I have no clean matching socks."

"Gotta go," said Anastasia, grabbing her jacket from the doorknob where it usually hung.

Outside, around the corner, she took the ski hat off. She found the comb that she had put in the pocket of her jeans, combed her hair up into the air again, and headed toward school — the long way so that she would pass Washburn Cummings's house.

The timing was just right. Washburn Cummings came dribbling through his front door just as Anastasia was walking past.

"Hello," she said, twitching her hips a little. She had practiced both the hello and the hips for quite a long time the night before.

Washburn Cummings stopped mid-dribble, stood still for a moment, and then tossed his invisible basketball with an absent-minded hook shot into a nearby tree.

"You stick your finger in a socket?" Washburn Cummings asked.

"What do you mean?"

"Your hair, girl. You look like you electrocuted yourself." He started to laugh. Often Anastasia's parents had told her that there is laughing *with* someone, and there is laughing *at* someone, and one is okay but the other is not. Washburn Cummings was definitely, she realized, laughing *at* her, and it was not okay, and she began to have a very serious stomachache.

"Halloween was all over last month," laughed Washburn Cummings. "It's not cool, baby, to wear your monster costume after Halloween's all finished. Noooot coooool." He retrieved the basketball from the air somewhere, bounced it a few times on the sidewalk, wiggled his hips, and began to dribble his way toward school.

Anastasia decided that she could not go to school that day. Her stomach hurt too much. She stuffed her hairdo back into the ski hat and stopped at the drugstore on her way home to buy a new tube of shampoo. It cost her entire week's allowance. As she was leaving Belden's Pharmacy, the new issue of *Cosmopolitan* caught her eye. "*Love — or Hate? Sometimes It's Hard to Tell,*" it said on the cover.

"You open it, you buy it, girlie," called Mr. Belden. He was watching her from the place where he measured out penicillin pills.

"Bug off, Mr. Belden," muttered Anastasia. She took her shampoo and her stomachache home, took a shower, washed her hair, and went to bed for the rest of the day.

"Call me if you throw up," said her mother. "I'll be doing the laundry."

But Anastasia didn't feel like throwing up. She sat on her bed and wrote, "I hate Washburn Cummings" in her notebook forty-three times until her stomachache went away. Then she read the *Boston Globe*, and found an article that told of a government research project which had found the average life span of a love affair to be five months.

"Mine was only three weeks," she thought. "But I'm young yet. And dumb. Dumb, dumb, *dumb* again."

Things I Love!	Things I Hate!
Making Lists	Mr. Belden (at the drugstore)
Mounds Bars	~~Boys~~
Writing Poems	Liver
My Room	Pumpkin Pie
My Wart	Mrs. Westvessel
Frank (my goldfish)	~~My Parents~~
Secret Bad Thoughts	Babies
Wedding Gowns	Boys
~~Washburn Cummings~~	Washburn Cummings

"Why did you have to give me the name Anastasia? None of the other kids can spell it, so when they have to vote for somebody by secret ballot, nobody ever votes for me. Like when I was nominated for Class Secretary, only four people voted for me, and the other twenty-two voted for Mary Ellen Bailey."

"The reason they didn't vote for you is because the Class Secretary has to have good handwriting. And your handwriting looks like hieroglyphics," said her father, looking up from the newspaper. "That time you tried to forge an absence excuse, you got caught right away, remember, because no parent — no adult, in fact — would get caught dead with handwriting like that."

"No adult would get caught dead with a name like Anastasia," Anastasia muttered, changing the subject back again, quickly, away from the handwriting and the absence excuse. "Why did you guys name me that?"

"Interesting question," said her father. "Choosing names is a fascinating procedure. Have you picked a name for the baby yet, Anastasia? What thought process did you go through to choose one?"

Anastasia pretended she hadn't heard his question. "If I didn't have such a dumb name, maybe Washburn Cummings would have liked me better," she said, even though the thought had not really occurred to her till that moment. But there was a possibility that it was true.

Her mother frowned and counted the stitches on her knitting needles. She was starting to make a baby sweater. "What's wrong with it, really? I think it's a lovely name."

"You have to pay *extra*, for pete's sake, to have it stenciled on a tee shirt. There are too many letters. That's *one* thing wrong with it."

"And *another* thing is that you can't make a nickname out of it. A nickname that ends in *i*." Anastasia glowered and picked some fuzz out of her belly button. She was sitting on the living room rug wearing last summer's bikini. She had been practicing standing on her head, until she fell and knocked over a lamp. Now she had a serious headache.

Her father scrunched his nose. "A nickname that ends in *i*? What on earth are you talking about?"

Anastasia sighed, lay on her back, and began raising her legs slowly one at a time. It was an exercise that ballet dancers did. It hurt a lot.

"The girls in my class started a club," she explained gloomily. "It's called the "*i* Club" and your name has to end in *i*. Everybody's in it but me. Jenni and Becki and Traci and Cindi and Suzi and Luci and . . ."

"Good grief," said her mother, and rolled her eyes upward. "Why would you want to belong to a club like that?"

"One. Because everybody's in it but me. Two. Because they're all getting tee shirts with their names on them."

"Well, look," said her father as he started in on the crossword puzzle, "if the tee shirt's that important, I'd be willing to fork over the extra money that a long name costs."

"Daddy," said Anastasia, sighing so hard that her shoulders lifted up and down. She stood up. "Look at me. I mean, look at my body."

He looked. "Not bad for ten years old," he said. "The legs are a little skinny, but I've seen worse."

"I mean look at my *chest*," said Anastasia. "And picture my name across it."

He looked for a long time. Finally he said, "You know, Anastasia, my mind works *verbally*. Your mother is the one with the visual imagination. Why don't you have her look at your chest?

"Does anyone know a four-letter word for ruler?" he asked, going back to the crossword puzzle.

"King," said Anastasia. "That's ridiculously easy."

"*The New York Times* wouldn't use *king*," her father grumbled, but he wrote it in lightly.

Anastasia went and stood in front of her mother. "Picture my name across my chest," she ordered.

"Wait till I finish this row." She knit for a minute. "Okay. Let me look."

Her mother looked at her chest for a long moment. Then she sighed. "Yes," she said. "I see what you mean."

"Into the *armpits*, right? The letters would go right into my armpits!"

Her mother nodded. "By the time you're sixteen you'll have a bigger chest," she said.

"Terrific. That's just terrific," said Anastasia. "By the time I'm sixteen I . . ."

"Czar!" interrupted her father. "I knew it couldn't be *king*. Not in *The New York Times*." He erased *king* and wrote in *czar*.

"As a matter of fact," he said, looking up. "Let me tell you something about your name. Anastasia was the youngest daughter of the czar of Russia. Czar Nicholas."

"Big deal," said Anastasia. "Did she have a tee shirt with her name on it?"

"And she was murdered."

52

"No kidding?"

"No kidding. The whole family was wiped out by the Bolsheviks, kids and all."

"Was she just a little kid?"

"I don't remember how old. A teen-ager. And they all got shot."

"Hey, that's cool."

Her father raised his eyebrows. "Well, I'm not sure I would call it cool. I don't suppose *they* thought it was cool at all. But here's an interesting thing: years later, some lady popped up out of nowhere and said she was Anastasia, that she hadn't been killed, really, just shot; and that later she escaped and grew up in hiding."

"Better than growing up in Hoboken, ha ha," said Anastasia, doing her Groucho Marx imitation, which her father ignored. He hated her Groucho Marx imitation. He thought his was better.

"I'm sorry," she said politely, apologizing for the Groucho Marx. "Was she really Anastasia?"

"I'm not sure that anyone ever really knew. Some people thought she was, some people thought she wasn't."

"But there was a *chance* that the czar's kid didn't die?"

"Sure. There was that possibility."

Anastasia thought. She thought for a long time. She assumed the lotus position, which was supposed to be good for thinking, even though you practically had to throw your hips out of joint to do it.

"Mom," she said slowly, "you didn't do natural childbirth when you had me, right?"

"Right."

"They knocked you out cold, right? Whonk. Out cold."

"Well, that's overstating it. They gave me an injection of something and I went to sleep briefly."

"So it's fair to say that you didn't actually *see* me being born?"

"You sound like a district attorney."

"Well, this is important. You didn't see me being born?"

"I felt you about to be born. I was put to sleep. I woke up a short time later and saw you being cleaned up. You looked very repulsive and you were screaming and you peed all over the nurse's hand."

"But for those few moments when you were asleep, there was *time* actually for them to switch babies on you."

Her mother groaned. "No way."

"You said that there were a few minutes . . ."

"Okay, so there were a few minutes when I was zonked out. Why would they switch babies? The only other baby born that day anyway, at that hospital, was Chinese. The parents had a restaurant over on Tyler Street in Boston. The father was terrifically handsome, I remember."

"But they could have switched babies! I might not even be yours!"

"The Chinese baby was a boy, come to think of it.

They named him Stanley. I always wondered why they named him Stanley."

"*I could be the real Anastasia!*"

Her father stood up. "I need a drink suddenly," he said. "I need a cold beer."

Before he went to the kitchen, he said, "Anastasia, it was 1918 when she was shot. If you are she, you are remarkably well-preserved."

"Rats," said Anastasia.

"Know what?" said her father, when he came back with his beer and let her slurp the foam. "When your grandmother's here at Thanksgiving, you can ask her about the czar, and about Anastasia. I wasn't born then. But she was a young woman. She'd remember."

"Daddy," Anastasia pointed out, using the kindliest voice she had, because she was talking about his mother, "Grandmother doesn't remember *anything*.

"She doesn't even remember *me*, for pete's sake," she muttered, forgetting the kindly voice. And she got that strange feeling again, the feeling she always had when she smelled medicine and other nursing home smells. It was a feeling of being scared and sad at the same time.

Things I Love!	Things I Hate!
Making Lists	Mr. Belden (at the drugstore)
Mounds Bars	~~Boys~~
Writing Poems	Liver
My Room	Pumpkin Pie
My Wart	Mrs. Westvessel
Frank (my goldfish)	~~My Parents~~
Secret Bad Thoughts	Babies
Wedding Gowns	Boys
~~Washburn Cummings~~	Washburn Cummings
My Name	All My Friends
	~~My Name~~

6

"The Macy's parade is the most boring thing I have ever seen," said Anastasia gloomily, "and I hate Thanksgiving."

Her mother opened the oven door, poked a fork into the turkey skin so that juice ran out and made a hissing noise. "You like turkey," she said.

"Yeah. But we could have turkey any time. I hate the Macy's parade, and after that I hate the football games, and also I hate pumpkin pie. Why do you have to make pumpkin pie on Thanksgiving? Is there a *rule* somewhere that you have to make pumpkin pie on Thanksgiving? If you want to know the truth, pumpkin pie smells like throw-up. It's gross."

"Anastasia Krupnik, *you* are being gross, and if you don't get out of this kitchen I'm going to throw something at you, maybe a pumpkin pie. Go. Go talk to your grandmother."

Anastasia muttered something as she left the kitchen.

"What did you say?" her mother called.

"Nothing," she called back. What she had muttered was, "I hate my grandmother."

Anastasia's grandmother was ninety-two. Nobody else's grandmother was ninety-two. Robert Giannini's grandmother was fifty; she played the Hammond Organ in a bar and lounge. She wore false eyelashes, Robert said, and called out, "All *riiiight*," when the TV showed closeups of the cheerleaders during Thanksgiving football games.

Jennifer MacCauley's grandmother was fat, worked in a bakery, and brought home all the unsold cookies at the end of each day. "Weight Watchers here I come," Jennifer MacCauley's grandmother always said, and laughed.

But Anastasia's grandmother was ninety-two and lived in a nursing home. The wrinkles on the side of her mouth were scabby. She talked with her mouth full, and what she said usually didn't make any sense, and there were food spots on the front of her dress.

She made Anastasia feel sad, and scared. Who needed *that*?

Anastasia wandered into the living room where her father was asleep on the couch with the *Boston Globe* open across his chest. In the corner by the window, her grandmother sat in a big chair, smoothing her dress across her lap over and over again with her thin hands. There were veins like cat's cradles pulled tight on the backs of her hands.

Anastasia sighed, sat down on the floor beside her grandmother, and said, "Hello, Grandmother," politely. She had already said hello four times since her father had brought her from the nursing home. But her grandmother forgot things.

The scary, clawlike hands smoothed her hair. Funny how soft and nice that felt. If she didn't look at the hands it was okay. If she just looked at her grandmother's moist, kind eyes, everything seemed almost okay.

"What's your name? You have such pretty hair."

"Anastasia." She had already told her that, again and again. Most people remembered their grandchildren's names, she thought angrily, and also their birthdays.

"My boy's hair is this color. His name is Myron," said the old woman.

For pete's sake, thought Anastasia. Myron is forty-five years old, asleep on the couch, and he's bald.

"Myron is a good boy," her grandmother said dreamily. "Better than his brothers. Myron always does his homework. Do you do your homework, little girl?"

"Mostly I do. But I don't like arithmetic much."

"Myron is the youngest, so I spoil him a little. His brothers are all so much older and they like to tease."

Anastasia glanced at her father and tried to imagine

him little, being teased by big brothers. It was hard. His mouth was open, and he was snoring a little; his glasses were pushed up on his forehead, scrunching his eyebrows. His feet stuck out beyond the end of the couch, almost touching the Swedish ivy that grew in the deep blue pot. Dr. Myron Krupnik was six feet four inches tall.

"Your little boy Myron is my father," she said politely to her grandmother, hoping that her grandmother would understand.

But her grandmother just stroked her hair some more with the skinny hands, and stared out through the window. "Do you have a brother, little girl?"

Anastasia sighed. "Not yet," she said. "But in March I will. My mother and father said that I could name him. What names do you like, Grandmother?"

Not that it mattered. Anastasia still had the name that she had chosen, written in the secret place in the back of her green notebook. She hadn't changed her mind about the name. It would serve the baby right. Also her parents.

"Sam," said her grandmother. "Sam is a good name."

Yuck, thought Anastasia. Sam.

The old woman leaned forward suddenly and whispered. "Sam's hands fit around my waist," she said, "and do you know, he can pick me right up and swing me around in the air? Sometimes he tickles me on the back of the neck with his mustache.

"But he doesn't come back anymore. I wonder

where Sam is," she said. "Do you know where he went?" She sat back stiffly, and looked around. "Is he invited? Is he coming today?"

"No," said Anastasia. "I guess he couldn't come."

Her grandmother looked back out through the window, leaning forward to see down the street. Her eyes were curious and almost happy. "He might come," she said. "Sometimes he surprises me."

She began to talk to herself, words that Anastasia didn't understand, and to smooth the lap of her dress once more. Anastasia got up and went back to the kitchen. Her mother was stirring gravy.

"Did you invite someone named Sam for dinner?" she asked her mother. "Grandmother says someone named Sam might come. There aren't enough places set."

Her mother tasted the gravy and added a little salt. "She's daydreaming," she told Anastasia. "Sam was your grandfather. He died before you were born. She forgets that."

"I forget it, too. Maybe I'm as bad as she is," said Anastasia, though she didn't believe it. "You want me to carry in the plates and put them on the table?"

"Sure. Put the one with the blue flowers at Grandmother's place. That's always been her favorite."

The plate with the blue flowers had a crack in it that was turning brown along its length. It had lasted a lot of Thanksgivings. But it was going to break one of these days.

"Are you going to have to mash up her turkey and

then we all have to watch her mushing it around, like last year?"

"Your eating habits aren't that terrific either, my friend," her mother said.

"She dribbles cranberry sauce on her dress, and she talks with her mouth full. I hate that."

Her mother didn't say anything.

"And she forgets my name. I hate that, too."

Her mother didn't say anything. She put mashed potatoes into a yellow bowl. Anastasia started to cry. A salt-flavored tear came down the side of her face and into the corner of her mouth; she tasted it with the tip of her tongue, and waited for the next one.

"I don't hate grandmother," she said in a voice that had to find its way out lopsided, around the tears. "But I hate it that she's so old.

"It makes my heart hurt."

Her mother took a paper napkin from the kitchen table, knelt on the floor beside Anastasia, daubed at her wet cheeks with the napkin, and put her arms around her.

"All of our hearts hurt," she said. They went together to wake up Anastasia's father, and the three of them helped the grandmother to the table, where they sat her in the best chair, the one with arms. They all smiled when the old woman recognized her favorite plate, touched the blue flowers fondly, and said, "For-get-me-nots."

Things I Love!	Things I Hate!
Making Lists	Mr. Belden (at the drugstore)
Mounds Bars	~~Boys~~
Writing Poems	Liver
My Room	Pumpkin Pie
My Wart	Mrs. Westvessel
Frank (my goldfish)	~~My Parents~~
Secret Bad Thoughts	Babies
Wedding Gowns	Boys
~~Washburn Cummings~~	Washburn Cummings
My Name	~~All My Friends~~
My Grandmother	~~My Name~~
My Friends	

"Hey sport, you're on vacation, right?" Dr. Myron Krupnik asked Anastasia one morning.

"Right. Christmas vacation. Goes till January third," said Anastasia, stuffing her jeans into a pair of heavy socks so that she could pull on her boots.

"Got any plans for this morning?"

"Well, I made a list." Anastasia pulled a crumpled piece of paper from her pocket and read it aloud. "Thursday morning: Make a snowman if there is enough snow. Start making Christmas presents. See if Mom will let me make cookies." She wrinkled her nose. "Mom said no to that. She's out of flour. Actually, I used up the flour myself, making paste the other day. We had five pounds of flour. Now we have about fourteen pounds of paste, and it's beginning to smell bad."

"Well," said her father, "*my* vacation doesn't start until day after tomorrow. But I only have to teach one class this morning. Do you want to come along?"

"Will it be boring?"

Her father adjusted his glasses so that he could look down his nose at her. "*Boring?* Dr. Krupnik's English 202, required for English majors, eighteenth and nineteenth century poetry, three prelims, four papers, and a final exam, *boring?*" He sighed. "Yes. It will probably be boring."

"Okay," said Anastasia, "I'll come. But wait while I change to my poetry outfit."

Anastasia's poetry outfit was quite simple. She put a black turtleneck shirt on with her jeans, replaced her owl's eye-shaped glasses with dark glasses, and undid her pony tail. She combed her hair straight and flat. If she had had time, she would have painted her fingernails crimson.

That was what the visiting lady poet who had come to their class had worn. She had also worn a cape. But Anastasia had no cape; she covered her poetry outfit with her green ski jacket, and walked with her father to the university.

She had never gone to one of her father's classes before. She had been to his office, in the same brick building, where his name — Dr. Krupnik — was impressively etched in a brass nameplate attached to the door. She had run her fingers over the letters, liking the way they felt, thought briefly about asking for an A. Krupnik nameplate for her own bedroom door at home, decided it would be ostentatious (a word she had written on page seven of her green notebook), at age ten, and discarded the idea. She would have a nameplate when her name was more important, she decided: maybe by the time she was twelve.

The classroom was not much different from the fourth grade classroom of the J. Henry Bosler Elementary School. There was no cage of smelly gerbils, no portrait of George Washington, no alphabet marching across the top of the blackboard, and no fire-resistant Christmas wreath. But it had the same large windows, the same blackboards, the same metal wastebasket, the same clock with nervous, jumpy hands, and the same smell of chalk dust and overflowing pencil sharpeners.

Someone had written "I work very hard for my Marx" on the board, but her father erased that with the side of his hand when they entered the room.

"We have about five minutes," her father said, "before it is feeding time at the zoo. Here, read this while we wait." He gave her a mimeographed poem called "I Wandered Lonely as a Cloud."

Anastasia sat down in one of the front-row desks and read the poem. It was not a difficult poem. It was easier to understand than some of the ones that her father wrote. There were only two words that she didn't understand: *jocund* and *pensive*, and she underlined them carefully the way Mrs. Westvessel had taught her to do. She could look them up when she got home. If they were any good, she could put them on the word list in her notebook.

The students began to enter the classroom. Anastasia was startled at their loudness — at the J. Henry Bosler Elementary School students were not allowed to shove the desks around, or talk to each other when lessons were starting; and although the issue hadn't been raised in the fourth grade, she suspected they would not be allowed to smoke cigarettes, which some of her father's students were doing — but she was pleasantly surprised that they were all wearing variations of poetry outfits, so she felt she would blend in nicely. She wished that she had Frye boots, though.

"Who's the midget, Dr. K?" asked one of the students, a boy. She thought it was a boy, at least; it was a little hard to tell, but the voice was rather deep for a girl.

Her father stood up. "Before we start, class, I would like you to meet my daughter, Anastasia, who is visiting today."

"All riiiggghht," said the girl in the desk next to Anastasia's, and smiled at her.

Dr. Krupnik lit his pipe. "Today we will continue with Wordsworth. Since Christmas vacation is upon us and we are busy, I gave you quite a simple assignment. Is it fair, or safe, to assume that you have all read and given some thought to an analysis of "I Wandered Lonely as a Cloud"?

Anastasia nodded gravely and said, "Yes." The rest of the class hooted and laughed. Mrs. Westvessel would have sent them all to the principal's office. Her father only grinned a little, and sighed.

"McAllister?" he said. "Let's hear from you. Tell us what you think of the poem."

The boy who had asked who the midget was groaned. "Frankly, Dr. K," he said, "I think it's a crock of shit." Then he sat up straighter, looked embarrassed, glanced at Anastasia, and mumbled, "I'm sorry."

Her father puffed on his pipe for a moment. "I'm sure my daughter has heard the word *shit* before," he said, "although I expect she is as surprised as I am to hear it in a classroom."

Anastasia giggled. Actually, she had heard it that very morning, from her own father, when he realized that his pen had leaked ink on the pocket of his favorite shirt.

"Would you explain why you find the poem offensive, McAllister?" her father asked.

The boy looked at his mimeographed sheet. "Well, like, look at lines fifteen and sixteen. I mean, like, it's not enough that he has to write about all those flowers fluttering around, but then he has to come out and tell us 'A poet could not but be gay'? Come on. And *jocund*. What's *that* mean?"

"Jocund means cheerful, McAllister," said Anastasia's father. "Surely you have access to a dictionary?

Would you *use* it occasionally, please?" Dr. Krupnik sounded annoyed.

McAllister slumped back in his desk. He cracked his knuckles. Anastasia winced. So did her father.

"Miss Eisenstein? Would you tell us, please, which line or lines convey to you the theme of the poem, and what that theme might be?"

A fat girl dressed entirely in black — a super-poetry-outfit — adjusted her glasses.

"Well, I couldn't pick out any one or two lines, you know? You have to look at it in its entirety. And then you see the dichotomy . . ."

Anastasia's father interrupted. "Remember, Miss Eisenstein, we sort of had a friendly agreement that you wouldn't use the word dictotomy in this class any morc? Because it has become a bit of a victim of overuse?"

The fat girl frowned. "Well, look at it this way, you know? Wordsworth is talking about two different things: like solitude, and also community? I mean, see how the flowers are all in a group, dancing, but in the last stanza the poet is lying on his couch all alone?"

That was interesting, Anastasia thought. Her father wrote "Solitude — Community" on the board.

"That is interesting, Miss Eisenstein," said her father. But he said it with the same voice that he used when Anastasia described in detail the plot of a television program. It meant that he didn't find it terribly interesting at all.

"Anyone else want to give it a try?" asked her father. "Miss Cameron?"

Anastasia turned around to look at the back of the classroom. A girl in the rear corner desk was at least six feet tall, dressed in a black leotard with a denim wraparound skirt tied loosely around her waist. Her hair was red and very, very long; it hung below the beginning of the skirt.

She yawned, unwrapped her thin leotarded legs from the legs of the desk, stretched her arms, and said, "To me the salient lines appear throughout the poem. 'Fluttering and dancing in the breeze.' 'Tossing their heads in sprightly dance.' 'The waves beside them dance.' 'And dances with the daffodils.' The whole thing flows, you know? Can you get with the flow? I'd say the theme is like movement as joy. Do you feel what I mean: 'movement as joy'?" The girl moved one of her thin arms across the air. The whole class watched her, puzzled.

"Ah, yes, Miss Cameron," said Anastasia's father. He wrote "Movement as joy" on the blackboard. "That's interesting. I'm not sure that Wordsworth would have known what you meant, or gotten with the flow, but it's, ah, interesting.

"Anyone else?" he asked. "Wilder? How about you?"

A heavyset boy with very curly hair had his head down on his desk. He raised his head and looked around with half-open eyes.

"Futility of life," he said.

There was a long silence. Finally Dr. Krupnik said, "Do you want to add anything to that, Wilder?"

"No."

"I find it fascinating, Wilder, that you have selected 'futility of life' to be the theme of the work of, so far, Pope, Gray, Cowper, Blake, and Burns. Now Wordsworth, too?"

"Yeah," said Wilder.

Anastasia's father wrote "futility of life" on the board.

"Others?" he asked.

The boy named McAllister called out, "Why don't you ask your daughter?"

Dr. Krupnik puffed on his pipe. Anastasia recognized it as a beginning-to-get-very-irritated style of puff.

"Because my daughter is not a registered member of this class," he said.

He paused for a long time and puffed again. "As a matter of fact," he said, finally, "let's call it a day. Go home, everybody, and have a good Christmas. *Read* over vacation, please. Read *anything*."

That seemed an odd thing to say, thought Anastasia. At home he was always saying to her, "Are you reading again? Don't you ever do anything but read?"

The students all shuffled to their feet and out of the classroom. Some of them said "Merry Christmas."

Someone called "Merry Christmas, Wilder!" Wilder was the only one who hadn't left. He had his head back down on the desk and appeared to be sound asleep. Maybe dead.

Anastasia held her father's hand as they walked home for lunch. She liked the feeling of his leather glove around her mitten. In a funny way that she didn't really understand, she felt bad for him.

"Daddy," she said shyly, "I think I understood a little bit of the poem. At least, I *liked* some parts of it."

He smiled and squeezed her hand. "What did you like?"

" 'The inward eye,' " she confessed. "I liked where it said about 'the inward eye.' "

He quoted the line as if it were an old friend. " 'The inward eye which is the bliss of solitude.' "

"Tell me what it means," said Anastasia. Inside, she pictured a head with a spooky eye.

"Well," said her father thoughtfully, " 'the inward eye' can mean memory. Solitude means being alone. And bliss means happiness. So what do you think the whole line means?"

She put it together like a puzzle. "Memory is the happiness of being alone?" she asked.

"Not a bad thought, is it?" asked her father, in a soft voice.

"No," said Anastasia, a little puzzled. "But my trouble is that I don't have very many memories yet. And

I'm not alone very much. So I guess I don't need 'the inward eye,' yet, to be happy."

He smiled at her.

"But probably I *will*, someday," she said. "Probably everybody does sometime, right, Daddy?"

"Right," he said. She could tell he was thinking.

"Daddy," she said, "I didn't understand some other things in your class. Like the boy named Wilder who was asleep. What did he mean when he said 'futility of life'?"

Her father thought about that. "Some people think that there's nothing to look forward to in life. Nothing important. Nothing that has any meaning for them.

"Feeling that way makes them bored and grouchy and lonely. Then they want to put a label on why they feel that way. Wilder's label is 'futility of life.' And he sleeps all the time in class because he stays up all night drinking beer and talking about how life has no meaning."

"That's dumb."

"Of course it's dumb." He squeezed her hand.

"You want to know something sad that I just thought of, though?" Anastasia asked.

"Sure."

"Grandmother. She doesn't have anything left to look forward to. *Grandmother* has 'futility of life.' Maybe she should go out and drink beer all night."

Her father looked thoughtful for a minute. Then he said, "No. Because your grandmother has something else that keeps her from being bored and grouchy and lonely. Can you guess what it is?"

Anastasia thought for a long time, about what her grandmother had. "Arthritis," she said finally, "and varicose veins. A pot of geraniums beside her bed at the nursing home, and twelve different kinds of pills. I don't think any of that's so terrific, for pete's sake."

"Nope," said her father. "None of that is terrific at all. But your grandmother has what we just talked about. She has memories. The people at the nursing home tell me that she lives in the past, and that she's happy."

" 'The inward eye'!" said Anastasia, understanding suddenly. "Grandmother has 'the inward eye'!"

" 'Which is the bliss of solitude,' " quoted her father, and tucked her hand into his coat pocket beside his own.

They were almost home. They walked along without saying anything for a moment.

"Daddy?"

"What?"

"I thought your class was kind of boring," Anastasia confessed.

"It was." He laughed. "It was hideously, horribly, *horrendously* boring."

"But Wordsworth was okay."

"Yeah," he said. "Good old Wordsworth. He's definitely okay."

Things I Love!	Things I Hate!
Making Lists	Mr. Belden (at the drugstore)
Mounds Bars	~~Boys~~
Writing Poems	Liver
My Room	Pumpkin Pie
My Wart	Mrs. Westvessel
Frank (my goldfish)	~~My Parents~~
Secret Bad Thoughts	Babies
Wedding Gowns	Boys
~~Washburn Cummings~~	Washburn Cummings
My Name	~~All My Friends~~
My Grandmother	~~My Name~~
My Friends	
Wordsworth	
Christmas	

"Nothing interesting ever, *ever* happens to me," said Anastasia gloomily. "No *wonder* I don't have any memories yet."

"What on earth do you mean? I can think of lots of interesting things that have happened to you," said her mother.

"Name three."

"When you were two years old you ate ant poison and had to have your stomach pumped."

"That's one. And I don't even remember it."

"Well, when you were four you wandered off when we were in Harvard Square. And finally I called the police, and when they finally found you, you were way down on Green Street, walking with an old lady who was wearing army boots and had a Tupperware bowl on her head."

"Yeah, that was neat. She said she always wore that bowl when she went out because it kept radioactivity from getting into her brain. She was going to take me home and we were going to live together and she said she would teach me to avoid all the filth and danger in the world. She needed me to help her wash the doorknobs in her apartment. She had to do them all three times a day."

"Well, *that* was sure an interesting thing that happened to you."

"It's only two. Name a third."

Her mother thought and thought. "The second grade field trip to the Franklin Park Zoo?"

"Yuck."

"Well, what sort of thing did you have in mind?"

"I was reading this newspaper at the drugstore. Just on the first page — the first page *alone* — I read about a man and his son in South America who were transported to another planet by a UFO; and a five-year-old girl in Idaho who had four kidneys, all of them working; and a pair of eight-year-old twins in New York who had lived all alone in an apartment for four months after their mother ran away with a guy who sold cosmetics door-to-door. And I didn't even get to read the second page because Mr. Belden told me that if I even *flicked* that newspaper open I had to pay for it."

"For that kind of reading I think I would have paid and flicked."

"I couldn't. I didn't have any money. Not only do I not have interesting things happen to me, but also I never have any money."

"Go ask your dad for your allowance. He's in the study looking through the closet for the Christmas tree decorations."

"I will in a minute. But tell me something, first: has anything interesting ever happened to *you?*"

"Like being taken to another planet? Nope."

"No, I don't mean like that. But how about — well, for example, did you ever have a love affair? After you were grown up?"

"Not since I married your dad."

"But before? Did you *before* you got married?"

Her mother blushed. "Anastasia, that is a very *personal* question."

"Well, you're my mother, for pete's sake. You're supposed to be able to ask your mother personal questions."

"Yes."

"Yes *what?*"

"Yes, I once had a love affair. Before I even met your father."

"With who? I mean with whom?"

"Oh, goodness, Anastasia, no one you know. His name was John. He was a lawyer in New York when I was an art student."

"Was he married so that you had to meet secretly and maybe there would be a detective watching?"

"Good heavens, of course not. He was just a young lawyer, not married, and I . . ."

"Handsome? Was he terrifically handsome?"

Her mother blushed again. "Yeah," she said, laughing a little. "He was terrifically handsome."

"And did you do wildly romantic, crazy things?"

"Sure."

"Like what?"

Her mother grinned. "Well, one time we drove all the way out to Montauk Point in the middle of the winter and found a place to spend the weekend, and we walked on the beach in a raging snowstorm. After that we had dinner and drank a lot of wine and listened to Beethoven on a little radio that had a lot of static. And we hugged and kissed a lot. Is that the kind of thing you want to know about, Anastasia?"

"Just romance. Just the romantic parts are what I want to know about."

"Well, here's a romantic part. Once he had to go to Charleston, South Carolina, on business. Some kind of legal thing he was doing. And he asked me, on the spur of the moment, to go along. So we flew to Charleston — it was spring, by then — and the whole city smelled like azaleas and gardenias. We stayed at a hotel where there were fresh flowers everywhere, so that every time, even now, when I smell those Southern spring flowers, I still think of that time. And that night, we had dinner in the hotel, and there was candlelight, and after dinner we had tea, and we were happy and laughing and we read each other's fortunes in the tea leaves."

"Yeah. That's romantic. What fortune did he give you?"

"He looked in my teacup and told me that I would be a good painter, and that he could see me ten years in the future, and I would be barefoot, with a smudge of paint on my ankle and another on my nose, and I would be laughing."

"That was nice. You liked that fortune, didn't you?"

"Yes. I liked it."

"And what was his?"

"Well, then I looked in his teacup and told him that I could see *him* in ten years, and he was a very successful lawyer, carrying a briefcase filled with important papers, and he was wearing a three-piece suit and being considered for a judgeship, and he had a big house in Scarsdale."

"And he liked that."

"He liked that."

"Then what?"

"Then we looked at each other and I started to cry." Anastasia was puzzled. Why would her mother *cry?* Then suddenly she understood.

"I know why. Because your fortunes didn't match."

"Right."

"And he cried, too."

"Nope. He was very sweet. Very sad. Very kind. And he said all the right things. But he didn't cry."

"Because men don't cry much."

"No. Men don't cry much."

"Daddy does, sometimes. He *always* cries when he hears that Sibelius violin concerto."

"Sweetie, that's one of the reasons I married your dad."

Anastasia understood that. "Yeah," she said. She looked at her mother. Her mother wasn't barefoot, because it was December; but she was wearing one green knee sock and one white knee sock, and there was a bit of orange paint on the white one; and there was another bit of orange paint on her chin. She was smiling, and she looked very, very beautiful to Anastasia. For a moment it didn't matter too much that in the middle, somewhere between the knee socks and the smile, was the baby.

"Daddy, I think love is one of the hardest things in the world to understand."

"Wait till you encounter calculus." Her father did his Groucho Marx eyebrow thing.

"Don't joke, Daddy. I really mean it. I need to start worrying about making myself some memories. I have to understand stuff."

"I'm sorry. You're right, Anastasia. Love is just about the hardest thing to understand. Maybe that's why there are painters and musicians and poets."

"And obstetricians," giggled Anastasia. "Can I have

my allowance? And have you found the Christmas tree decorations? And did you ever have love affairs?"

"Yes. No. Yes." He gave her three quarters. "What kind of box are they in? Do you remember?"

"A Jordan Marsh box, kind of smashed in on one corner. Tell me about your love affairs."

"Good grief. I had lots. Poets always do. They read poetry to women, usually young, wide-eyed women, and then the women get all misty-eyed and lick their lips a lot and next thing you know they say, 'I love you.' Happens all the time, to poets."

"There's the box, under that old sweat shirt." Anastasia pointed. "Did you really love any of them?"

"Nope. Pretended, though. Well, maybe I really loved one."

"Annie?"

"How did you know about Annie?"

"Your book. It says, 'To Annie.' "

"Yeah," said her father. "I'd forgotten that. Annie was pretty wonderful. But she ran off to someplace, Guatemala, I think, and broke my heart."

"What does a broken heart feel like when you're a grownup?"

"Stomachache. Lasts about six months. If you're a poet, you get some good poetry out of a broken heart, though."

"Did you ever have a love affair after you and Mom got married?"

"Sure. With your mom. It's still going on."

"Come on, Daddy. Be honest. With anybody else?"

"Nope. Because I've never had any clean underwear. Come on, kiddo, let's put up the Christmas tree."

"Grandmother, would you like to tell me about Sam?"

Anastasia was sitting beside her grandmother on the living room couch after Christmas dinner. She had tried and tried and tried to think of things to talk about. She had talked about the lights on the tree; she had talked about her best present, a record player, and had tried to show her grandmother some of her favorite albums; she had tried to talk about the czar; and she had tried to talk about school. But her grandmother had only seemed puzzled and confused, nodding her head up and down with a questioning look. She held Anastasia's hand tightly, as if she were frightened.

"Maybe you would like to tell me about you and Sam when you were young," suggested Anastasia again.

Her grandmother smiled suddenly. "Is Sam here?" she asked, looking around.

"No," said Anastasia gently. "But tell me about him."

"He calls me Ruthie. 'Ruthie with the red, red hair.' Isn't that silly?"

Anastasia looked at her grandmother's white hair.

She felt sad, even though it was Christmas. "No," she said. "It isn't silly."

"I made him a shirt for his birthday. It was a secret. I never sewed on it when he was around. I kept it hidden away. I did every seam twice, by hand — such a soft, blue shirt. And when his birthday came, I made a special dinner, but I told him that I had no gift. I pretended to be very sorry, and of course he knew that we didn't have any money. It costs so much to feed the boys — goodness, how the boys eat! Are they here? Have they had dinner?"

Anastasia wasn't sure what to say. "Yes," she answered finally, "they've had dinner."

"Well, then I brought out the shirt! And my goodness, wasn't Sam surprised! He put it right on, and gave me a hug even though I was so big because the baby was about to be born, and do you know what?"

"What?"

"That night, that very night, the baby came. Two weeks early. So Sam was wearing his birthday shirt when the littlest one, Myron, was born, right on his father's birthday! I looked up and saw Sam holding the baby against the blue shirt, and he told me we had another boy. That was such a happy time!"

"What a happy, happy time," the old woman said softly, stroking Anastasia's hand.

" 'The inward eye,' " thought Anastasia, "that makes you feel happy, and not so all alone. Good old Wordsworth."

Suddenly her grandmother sat up straight, looked

around, and said politely, "Little girl, I would like to go home now. I would like to be with Sam."

"Grandmother, I wish you could go and be with him," said Anastasia, and then felt frightened by what she had said. She looked across the room to where her mother and father were sitting and listening, and she knew that it had been all right, to say it. She knew that they were wishing it, too.

"Merry Christmas, Grandmother," she called softly after the car as her father took her grandmother back to the nursing home. Funny, how it had never felt sad to say Merry Christmas before.

Things I Love!	Things I Hate!
Making Lists	Mr. Belden (at the drugstore)
Mounds Bars	~~Boys~~
Writing Poems	Liver
My Room	~~Pumpkin Pie~~
My Wart	Mrs. Westvessel
Frank (my goldfish)	~~My Parents~~
Secret Bad Thoughts	Babies
Wedding Gowns	Boys
~~Washburn Cummings~~	Washburn Cummings
My Name	~~All My Friends~~
My Grandmother	~~My Name~~
My Friends	
Wordsworth	
Christmas	
My Parents	
Memories	

"Daddy, I need to know a word."

"Mmmmmmm?"

"What's a word that means, well, someone who changes his mind all the time?"

"How many letters?"

"Daddy, I'm not doing a crossword puzzle, for pete's sake. I just want to know a word to describe that. Someone who thinks one thing one day and another thing the next day."

"Well, let me think. *Mercurial*'s a pretty good word. Someone like that has a mercurial temperament."

Anastasia said that to herself a few times. Mercurial temperament. Mercurial temperament. It sounded pretty good. She got out her green notebook and wrote, on page two, under "These are the most important things that happened the year that I was ten": "I began to have a mercurial temperament."

She put the green notebook away and wandered into the little pantry between the kitchen and the dining room. Her mother was there, trying to put a curtain rod up over the little window. They had already taken all the dishes out of the pantry and painted the walls pale blue. It was going to be the baby's bedroom. Anastasia thought it a very peculiar sort of bedroom and she felt a little sorry for the baby, who would be lying in a little crib looking up at glass-doored cupboards that had once held cocktail glasses. But her mother had made some nice curtains for the little window; the curtains had blue and green cross-eyed unicorns on them.

Anastasia looked cross-eyed briefly at the curtains. She was pretty good at it, but it made her eyes hurt. Robert Gianinni could look cross-eyed all the time, just by taking off his glasses, and he said it didn't make his eyes hurt at all; but he couldn't *see* when he was cross-eyed.

"I have a mercurial temperament," Anastasia said to her mother.

"You also have a terribly dirty shirt on," her mother said. "Don't you have any clean clothes?"

"Yes, but I hate all my clean shirts. This is my favorite shirt. I'll save the clean ones for school. This is okay for Saturday."

Her mother hammered a nail into the window

frame, said "ouch," and the bent nail fell onto the floor. Her mother put her thumb into her mouth.

"Don't you agree that I have a mercurial temperament?"

"Tell me what it means," said her mother, sucking her thumb.

"It means someone who changes her mind a lot."

"What have you changed your mind about?"

Anastasia hoisted herself up on the countertop and sat with her legs dangling. What a strange bedroom, she thought again. With a sink and everything.

"Well, just for an example, do you remember that at Thanksgiving I told you I hated pumpkin pie?"

"Mmmmm."

"Did you notice at Christmas that I ate a whole lot of pumpkin pie?"

"Yes," said her mother thoughtfully. "As a matter of fact I *did* notice that. Christmas night, very late, I sneaked into the kitchen to get something to eat, and what I wanted was a piece of pumpkin pie. And it was all gone. You ate all the whipped cream, too."

"Yeah. Mercurial temperament."

Her mother took another nail from the package and began to line it up on the window frame.

"And remember I loved Washburn Cummings? And then after a while I *hated* Washburn Cummings? Guess what."

"What?"

"Now I'm starting to love him again."

Her mother took a whack with the hammer and

another bent nail fell to the floor. "Damn," she said softly.

"And for a while I wanted to be a Catholic? And then I didn't want to?"

"Do you want to be a Catholic again?"

"No," said Anastasia glumly. "But now I'm starting to think about being a Hare Krishna."

"A *what?*" Her mother took out another nail.

"Hare Krishna. You know those guys who wear yellow robes and have shaved heads and they dance around in Harvard Square saying 'Hare Krishna, Hare Krishna'?" Anastasia hopped down from the countertop and began to dance, shuffling her feet, around the little pantry. She bumped into the folded crib, which toppled against her mother, who was about to swing the hammer. Another nail fell on the floor.

"*Anastasia,*" said her mother, angrily.

"Sorry," said Anastasia, and jumped up onto the countertop again. "And my name. Sometimes I hate my name and sometimes I think it's okay. Those Hare Krishna guys, they all get to take new names."

Her mother sighed, set the crib upright, and took out another nail.

Anastasia kicked her feet against the wooden drawers under the counter. What a weird bedroom, she thought, with drawers that used to hold tablecloths. Thunk thunk thunk. A little chip of white paint fell onto the floor beside the bent nails.

Her mother held the nail in her left hand, took a deep breath, and aimed the hammer with her right.

Thunk thunk. Anastasia kicked some more paint off the drawer, and said, "If you're not real careful you could hit the windowpane."

Her mother hit the windowpane with the hammer. The glass shattered and fell into the little sink.

Her mother stood very still for a moment. Then she said, very quietly, "If you don't get out of here, Anastasia, I am going to kill you."

Anastasia jumped down from the counter and shuffled away, doing her Hare Krishna dance. "I thought you liked me," she said. "You must have a mercurial temperament, too."

She wandered into the kitchen where her father was slicing some garlic cloves. There was company coming for dinner.

"Yuck," said Anastasia. "Those smell terrible."

Her father looked grouchy. "*Where* is your mother?" he asked. "Why do I seem to be preparing this dinner?"

"She's hammering, and she's very mad."

"Well, I'm not too cheerful myself. I don't know how to fix a leg of lamb. I'm an English professor. Go tell her if she doesn't want to cook we can call off the dinner party."

"I can't go tell her. I'm not speaking to her, maybe not ever again. Can I eat with you guys tonight?"

"No." Her father poked the sliced garlic into the lamb a lot harder than it needed to be poked.

"Why not?"

"Because it's a grownups' party. Probably there

won't be any food anyway. At least she made the hors d'oeuvres before she copped out. We can eat hors d'oeuvres. As a matter of fact, if you change out of that crummy shirt you can pass the hors d'oeuvres."

"I love this shirt. It has good memories attached to it. Bear in mind that I am someone who doesn't *have* a whole lot of memories yet."

"That shirt has the memory of a cheeseburger on the sleeve. Don't you have any decent clothes? Didn't your mother buy you a dress once?"

Anastasia ignored him. She lay down on the kitchen floor, on her back, and began breathing very loudly and quickly, huffing and puffing.

"Should I call an ambulance? Are you having an epileptic seizure?"

Anastasia stopped huffing, sat up, and looked at him with disdain. "Daddy, you of all people should recognize Lamaze breathing. I'm doing exactly what you and Mom do when you practice to have the baby. 'Transitional breathing.'"

He patted some flour into the leg of lamb and looked at her with interest. "I'll be darned. I never realized it sounded so grotesque."

She lay down again and puffed for a while. "Do I have it right?"

"Sounds right to me. You've really been paying attention when your mother and I practice, haven't you?"

"Yeah," she admitted. "I only pretended I wasn't

interested. Actually I was listening all the time. And I looked through the book, too."

"Hmmmm," he said. He was scowling at the leg of lamb.

"Daddy, do you want to know *why* I'm doing the breathing?"

"Sure. Why?"

"Because I want to be there, the same as you, when the baby is born."

Her father went to the refrigerator, poured himself a beer, gave her a sip of the foam, and sat down at the kitchen table.

"You can't, sport," he said regretfully. "I wouldn't mind, and I'm sure your mom wouldn't mind. But the hospital has strict rules. No kids in the delivery room except the kid who is being delivered."

"*Why?*"

He sipped his beer and rubbed his beard. "Well, my guess is that it has to do with size. Everything is scaled to adult size. You're just not big enough, Anastasia. The hospital gown wouldn't fit you; it would drag on the floor. You're too short to stand by the delivery table; you'd bump your cute nose, sweetie."

"Daddy, that is the dumbest thing I have ever heard you say. *Ever.*"

"Why is it dumb?"

"Have you ever heard of midgets?"

"Of course I've heard of midgets."

"Don't you think midgets have *babies?* For pete's

sake, do you think they tell midgets, 'Sorry, but we can't let you in the delivery room even though you're having a baby because you'd bump your cute little *nose*,' for pete's sake?"

He made a face, and touched her nose fondly. "You're absolutely right. It was a dumb thing to say. It doesn't have anything to do with size. It's just a rule. And we have to go along with it."

"You mean you won't even try to talk them into letting me watch?"

"No, sport. You can see the baby after he's born. But not during."

"*Traitor*. I hope your dinner party turns out terrible."

Anastasia glowered at her father and stomped out of the kitchen. In the pantry, her mother was kneeling on the floor and touching up the chipped paint with a small brush.

"Don't you dare come stomping in here that way, Anastasia," said her mother. "I have just three weeks to get this room ready for the baby and I can't spend three weeks repairing your damage."

So Anastasia stood in the center of the dining room, next to the table which was already set for the dinner, and called in her loudest voice, "Just for the record, everybody. I had *almost* changed my mind about that baby. I had *almost* begun to like that baby. I had *almost* begun to like the idea of having a brother living in the pantry, and I was even *about* to offer to maybe change his diapers occasionally. But just for the record for pete's sake, you guys shouldn't mess around with someone who has a mercurial temperament like mine, because just for the record I have absolutely changed my mind, and I do *not* like that baby at *all*."

Then she stomped noisily into her room, slammed the door, and scowled at Frank, who came to the side of his bowl, stared at her solemnly, and moved his lips in a silent blurp.

"Shut up, Frank," said Anastasia.

She rummaged in her desk and found the green notebook. Then she leafed through the last pages until she found the secret page on which she had written the name for the baby. It was still as terrible a name as it had been the very first day that she heard it. That had been the day last September when she had walked past Washburn Cummings and his friends as they stood on the street corner near the J. Henry Bosler Elementary School. They were singing. As Anastasia walked by, one of the boys had said "Shhhhh" and they had stopped singing. But they had started again when she was past, and she had stopped, knelt, pretended to tie her shoe, and listened to the song. It had a lot of verses, and she didn't understand all of them, but they were all about a man with a very peculiar, very terrible name.

Now she looked at the name where she had written it on the corner of the page in pencil. Carefully she went over the letters with a red marking pen.

The name was "One-Ball Reilly."

Things I Love!	Things I Hate!
Making Lists	Mr. Belden (at the dragstore)
Mounds Bars	~~Boys~~
Writing Poems	Liver
My Room	~~Pumpkin Pie~~
My Wart	Mrs. Westvessel
Frank (my goldfish)	~~My Parents~~
~~Secret Bad Thoughts~~	Babies
Wedding Gowns	~~Boys~~
~~Washburn Cummings~~	~~Washburn Cummings~~
My Name	~~All My Friends~~
My Grandmother	~~My Name~~
My Friends	My Parents
Wordsworth	Hospital Rules
Christmas	
~~My Parents~~	
Memories	
Washburn Cummings	
(maybe!)	

10

Anastasia woke up, reached one arm out from her bed to her desk, and tapped some fish food into Frank's bowl.

Frank never slept, as far as she could tell; and he liked to eat all the time. On one page of her green notebook she had listed all the words that she could think of to describe Frank's appetite: the list began with *huge* and ended with her favorite, *indefatigable*, and it even included *humungus* although her father said that was not a real word.

Frank blurped silently at her, flipped his tail, and swam around the bowl catching the bits of food as they floated down.

Something felt very strange. Something was missing. Anastasia sat up in bed and looked around her room. Sometimes the Scotch tape dried out and her orangutan poster fell off the wall; but it was still there. Her Red Sox cap was on the lampshade where it always was. Her arithmetic book was on the floor, where she had left it.

Something was so definitely missing that she took her legs out from under the covers and counted her toes. They were all there.

Then she began to count her fingers. When she got halfway through her fingers she realized what had happened.

"Mom! Daddy!" Anastasia yelled. "My wart is gone!"

She pulled back the covers of her bed and looked at the sheets. No small pink wart. It had simply disappeared as magically as it had come. Her left thumb felt naked.

She could hear her parents talking in the kitchen. She could smell coffee.

"Mom? Daddy?" she called. "Did you hear me? My wart is gone!"

Hastily she opened her green notebook to page two, and wrote, "I have no wart all of a sudden."

"Don't you guys even *listen* when I yell something important, for pete's sake?" Anastasia said, going into the kitchen where her parents were sitting at the table in their bathrobes. Her mother's stomach, she noticed suddenly, was huge. Humungus.

Both of her parents looked very sad.

"You don't have to feel bad for me or anything,"

said Anastasia. "It's not that big a deal. And probably someday I'll grow another one."

"Sweetie," said her father. "The nursing home just called. Your grandmother died last night."

" 'Ruthie with the red, red hair. Ruthie with the red, red hair.' " Anastasia said that over and over again, to herself; and she started to cry.

"I remember her sitting there in the big chair at Christmas," Anastasia said, through her tears.

"And the other weekend, remember? She liked those little cakes so much, when she was here that day? Remember that?"

Her parents nodded.

"And for pete's sake, she *wanted* to be with Sam, she said that, remember that she said that? And now I suppose she is, so I can't figure out why I feel like this. It's just that I remember how she used to touch my hair, and her hands felt soft; and I remember her eyes, how she looked at me sometimes, even though she couldn't even remember my name, for pete's sake; she still looked at me and rubbed my hair, and I remember how nice it felt . . ."

Anastasia cried and cried.

"I'm getting *memories*, all of a sudden!" she sobbed. "And they don't *feel* good!"

"And I wish I'd been nicer to her and not got so mad when she didn't know who I was." Anastasia wept.

She blew her nose on a paper napkin.

"It didn't hurt, did it, when she died?"

"No," said her father. "Her heart just stopped beating. She died of old age. Her time for living was simply over."

"Like my wart."

"Well," said her father, "maybe a little like your wart."

"You don't think I was stupid for crying, do you?"

"Goodness, Anastasia," her mother said. "Your dad and I both cried before you woke up. Look in the wastebasket. A whole batch of paper napkins crumpled up."

"I'll be back in a minute. I want to write something down."

In her green notebook, at the end of the list of important things that happened the year that she was ten, Anastasia wrote, "I have no grandmother all of a sudden."

Then she wrote, "But I have an inward eye, for the first time."

Late that morning, Anastasia went with her father to the Riverview Nursing Home.

"I don't want to see grandmother dead," she said to him when he asked her to come along.

"No," he told her. "You won't. Grandmother's body has been taken away. But the people at the nursing home want us to come and get her things. I suppose they have someone waiting for her room."

So she went along. She had been to the nursing home before, to visit her grandmother, but she had never liked it much. The name Riverview was a lie.

The Charles River was close by, but there was no view of it from the nursing home. From the window of her grandmother's room there was only a view of the underside of a fire escape, and one side of a Lutheran church.

"Grandmother must have hated looking at a fire escape all the time," Anastasia said when they went into the room and she saw the view again.

"I think," said her father, "that from her bed she could probably see the sky."

Anastasia lay down very straight and flat on the bare mattress of her grandmother's bed. She looked through the window and felt better.

"Yes," she said. "She could definitely see the sky."

"Would you help me, sweetie?" asked her father. "There are just these few things in the bureau. Let's pack them into the suitcase."

So Anastasia helped her father fold the clothes that still smelled like her grandmother: like soap and powder and lilac cologne. It made them both feel sad.

"I remember that she was wearing this sweater at Christmas," said Anastasia, rubbing the wool of the gray sweater against her cheek.

"She was wearing this nightgown when I came to see her last Sunday," said her father, looking at a folded gown of yellow flannel.

"What's this?" asked Anastasia, taking a shoebox from the top drawer. She opened it and looked inside. "Look! The paperweight that I made for her in first grade!"

She took out the little clay paperweight painted with tulips.

"And look! My school pictures!"

She took out the small photographs, three of them: first, second, and third grades. In the first grade picture, her front teeth were missing. In the second grade picture, her hair was a mess and her new front teeth made her look like a chipmunk. The third grade picture wasn't too bad, she thought, looking at it. "Hello, little girl," she said, imitating her grandmother. "What's your name?"

Her father took a gold ring from the box. "This was her wedding ring," he said. Anastasia slipped it onto her finger; it almost fit. Her grandmother had had small, thin hands.

"Who's that? It looks like you, with funny clothes." She took a photograph from her father's hands.

"That was my father. That was Sam."

The man had her father's face, but without the beard; he had a neatly-trimmed mustache, and a stiff collar. He had a nice, serious sort of smile.

"He was a good father, wasn't he, Daddy?"

"Yes," said her father. "He was a very good father."

"Grandmother sure loved him."

"She sure did."

"Boy," said Anastasia, "you know what I wish? I wish that everybody who loved each other would die at exactly the same time. Then nobody would have to miss anyone."

"Well," said her father slowly, "it just doesn't work

that way. It just doesn't seem to work that way very often."

They packed the rest of her grandmother's things: her glasses, the gold pin that she had worn on her dress at Thanksgiving and Christmas, her stockings, and a pair of soft woolen gloves. It didn't take very long.

Anastasia thought of her own room, and about the time when she had decided to leave home, and had packed in her father's US Navy bag. There were so many things in her room that she had had to leave most of them behind.

She wondered how it happened that when you were ninety-two you didn't have very many things left.

"When I'm old," she said, "I would like to keep my favorite things, like my orangutan poster and my Red Sox cap. And Frank, of course. If I have to go to a nursing home, would you make sure that I still have those things?"

"When you're old, sport," her father said, "I won't be around anymore."

"Oh. I forgot. Well, I'll have to tell my children, I guess." Anastasia reminded herself to write that down in her green notebook: "Things That I Want To Take To The Nursing Home When I Am Old."

"Is there anything special that *you* want to have around when you're old? Because you should tell me, and I'll write it down," she said to her father.

"Just one," he said with a smile. "Your mother."

They snapped the suitcase closed and looked around

the empty room. There was no sign of her grandmother left except the faint scent of powder and cologne. Anastasia lay down on the bed once more, flat on her back.

"Daddy, were there stars last night?"

"Yes. It was a very clear night. Millions of stars."

"Well, I feel absolutely sure that when Grandmother died she was looking at the sky and seeing millions of stars. Probably she was even smiling."

"And thinking of Sam," said her father.

"Yes. Thinking of Sam."

A nurse appeared at the door of the room and looked inside. Anastasia sat up quickly, feeling guilty because she had her shoes on the bed.

"Dr. Krupnik?" said the nurse.

"Yes?"

The nurse smiled. "Your wife just called. You'd better go right home. Your baby's on the way."

"For pete's sake," said Anastasia. "Everything's happening all at once. I think my wart must have caused it."

Things I Love!	Things I Hate!
Making Lists	Mr. Belden (at the drugstore)
Mounds Bars	~~Boys~~
Writing Poems	Liver
My Room	~~Pumpkin Pie~~
My Wart	Mrs. Westvessel
Frank (my goldfish)	~~My Parents~~
Secret Bad Thoughts	Babies
Wedding Gowns	~~Boys~~
~~Washburn Cummings~~	~~Washburn Cummings~~
My Name	~~All My Friends~~
~~My Grandmother~~	~~My Name~~
My Friends	~~My Parents~~
Wordsworth	Hospital Rules
Christmas	
~~My Parents~~	
Memories (esp. of my wart)	
Washburn Cummings (maybe!)	
My Late Grandmother	
My Parents	

11

The telephone rang late in the afternoon while Anastasia was alone in the apartment.

Once she had made an anonymous phone call to Washburn Cummings, to ask him if his refrigerator was running. But Washburn Cummings had answered the phone in a fake deep voice, and said, "For whom does this bell toll?" which threw her timing off, so that she had hung up giggling in embarrassment.

She had always, since then, wanted to answer the phone by saying, "For whom does this bell toll?" but her nerve always failed at the last moment.

It did again. She picked up the receiver and said, "Hello."

It was Mrs. Westvessel.

It made Anastasia feel very creepy to be talking to Mrs. Westvessel on the telephone. For some reason she didn't like to think of Mrs. Westvessel eating, or going shopping, or watching television, or being asleep. Teachers belonged only in front of a classroom, saying the spelling words in a loud, clear voice, or telling someone to turn around and sit up straight.

She also didn't like to think of Mrs. Westvessel as having any first name except Mrs.; so it felt very creepy to hear the voice say, "Anastasia, this is Dorothy Westvessel."

"Oh," said Anastasia. "Hello."

"Anastasia, when you were absent from school today, I thought it was just because you had a cold. Yesterday you were sniffling a little."

Anastasia couldn't think of anything to say, except, "Oh," again.

"But the evening paper just came, dear, and I saw that your grandmother had passed away. I called to tell you how sorry I am about that."

"Well," said Anastasia in a small voice, "she was very, very old."

"Yes, I know. But last year my mother died, and *she* was almost as old as your grandmother. And it made me feel very sad anyway, because I loved her. I know you must be feeling sad."

"Yes," Anastasia said. "I am."

"Well, I'll let you go, dear. But don't worry about your schoolwork. We all missed you in school today, but nothing very important happened. We had a film about Eskimos."

"Mrs. Westvessel?"

"Yes, dear?"

"My mother's at the hospital because she's having a baby today."

"Well, Anastasia! My goodness! You are certainly having a day of important events, and when you get back to school we will have lots to talk about!"

Anastasia said good-by politely, and Mrs. Westvessel said good-by politely; and Anastasia went to her room, found her green notebook, and crossed Mrs. Westvessel off the list of THINGS I HATE.

"I am most heartily sorry that I wished Mrs. Westvessel would get pimples," Anastasia confessed aloud to the empty apartment. She really *felt* sorry, too, and thought briefly that she might have been an okay Catholic after all.

She flipped the pages of her notebook and looked at the baby's name. Good old One-Ball Reilly Krupnik; Anastasia hoped that he was coming along all right, getting born.

Maybe, after all, it wouldn't be too bad, having a brother. Anastasia wandered into the little pantry room. Her mother had replaced the broken pane of glass, carefully puttying the edges; and the unicorn curtains were in place. The crib was set up, and there was a folded blue blanket in it. In the drawers that had once held tablecloths, the little clothes were folded and stacked. She picked up a tiny undershirt, unfolded it, and wondered how anybody could possibly be so small.

"For pete's sake, One-Ball," Anastasia said aloud to the empty room, "you are going to be revoltingly helpless if you are that little.

"I suppose," she said, looking at the baby carriage that stood in a corner of the dining room, "that I would be willing to take you for walks, maybe past Washburn Cummings's house. But I am absolutely not under any circumstances *ever* going to change your diapers."

"Anastasia!" Her father came through the front door of the apartment. "It's a boy!"

"Daddy," said Anastasia very patiently, "I *know* that."

Her father looked at her for a moment, and grinned. "Of course you do. I forgot. I need coffee. No, I need a beer. It was terrific. Your mother was terrific, and the baby is terrific. He weighs eight pounds and four ounces. Or maybe it's four pounds and eight ounces. No, I guess it's the way I said it first. I really need a beer."

Anastasia got him a beer and sipped the foam before she gave him the glass.

"Relax," she said, "and tell me about it. Did Mom do the breathing right?"

"Exactly right. And I didn't faint. For a minute I thought I was going to faint. But I didn't."

"Daddy, why would you *faint*? That's ridiculous."

"Of course it's ridiculous. Why would a grown man faint? The baby looks like you, Anastasia."

"Was he repulsive and screaming and did he pee on the nurse's hand?"

"That's exactly what he looked like and what he did. But then later, when he was all cleaned up and asleep, he looked terrific and he looked just like you. Same color hair."

"Freckles? Does he have freckles?"

Her father thought. "No," he said. "I didn't notice any freckles."

"He didn't get my *wart*, did he?"

"No. No wart."

"Good. Maybe when he's older he'll get his own wart."

"Come on. I came home to get you and take you back to the hospital so you can see Mom and the baby."

They stopped at the drugstore on the way to the hospital.

"I need a box of your best cigars," Anastasia's father said to Mr. Belden. "My wife just had a baby boy."

Mr. Belden leaned across the counter and shook his hand. "Congratulations," he said. Then he reached down to shake Anastasia's hand. "Congratulations to you, too, little girl. That's quite an accomplishment, to have a new brother." He took a foil-wrapped chocolate cigar from the candy counter and gave it to her.

"I happen to know that you like Mounds bars best,"

Mr. Belden said to Anastasia, "but today you'll have to make do with a chocolate cigar, because of the baby. Compliments of Belden's Pharmacy."

"Thank you," said Anastasia in surprise.

Back in the car, Anastasia took her green notebook from the glove compartment, turned to THINGS I HATE, and crossed out Mr. Belden's name.

Then she turned to the very last page, which was blank, and wrote something very carefully, very private, as a surprise. It made her feel good to write it.

In the hospital room, her mother was sitting up in bed, smiling. In a little crib beside her bed, the baby lay on his back with his eyes closed tight. Anastasia looked at him carefully. Yellow hair. No freckles. No warts. He didn't smell bad; he smelled clean and powdery. He wasn't crying.

"He's not a bad baby, for pete's sake," said Anastasia. She touched his curled-up hand; in his sleep, the baby opened his fist and wrapped his fingers around her thumb.

"Hey," said Anastasia in surprise. "I really like him!"

Her parents were smiling.

"Does he wet his diapers a whole lot?" Anastasia asked suspiciously.

"He's only five hours old," said her mother, "so I haven't had time to conduct an exhaustive study. But in all honesty, Anastasia, I have to tell you that I think he will probably wet his diapers a lot."

Anastasia sighed. "Well," she said, finally. "I can

tell that this baby is going to be a lot of work. So probably I will be willing to change his diapers occasionally.

"Only *wet* ones, though. Nothing else."

"Fair enough," said her mother.

"Have you picked out his name?" asked her father.

"Have I picked out his name?" said Anastasia. "What kind of dumb question is that? Of *course* I've picked out his name. But wait a minute; I want to write something down.

"Give me back my hand, please," she said politely to her brother, and took her thumb gently out of his fist. In her green notebook, under THINGS I HATE, she crossed out "BABIES."

Then she turned to the last page of her notebook, to what she had written in the car, and tore it out carefully. She laid the sheet of paper on the baby, on top of the white blanket that covered the little mound of his body and curled-up legs. She watched as the paper moved a tiny bit, up and down.

"Look," Anastasia whispered, awed. "Look how he breathes."

The paper said: "Someone Special: Sam."

"Hi, Sam," she said.

"Hi, Sam," said her mother.

"Hi, Sam," said her father.

"You know what?" said Anastasia, after a moment. "There's absolutely nothing left on my 'Things I Hate' list except liver, for pete's sake. I guess I'll always hate liver."

"Gee, Anastasia," said her father solemnly, "that's too bad, because that's what I was planning to give you for dinner tonight."

Anastasia took her foil-wrapped cigar out of her pocket. Very slowly she removed all of the foil. Then she put the cigar into her mouth and chewed on it, frowning, briefly. Finally, she took it out of her mouth, wiggled her eyebrows up and down, Groucho Marx style, flicked an imaginary ash from her cigar, and said, "Say the secret word and you win a hundred bucks."

"And the secret word is not *liver?*" asked her father, wiggling his own eyebrows.

"Nope."

"*Steak?*"

Anastasia grinned. "With mushrooms," she said.

Things I Love!	Things I Hate!
Making Lists	~~Mr. Bolden (at the drugstore)~~
Mounds Bars	~~Boys~~
Writing Poems	Liver
My Room	~~Pumpkin Pie~~
My Wart	~~Mrs. Westvessel~~
Frank (my goldfish)	~~My Parents~~
Secret Bad Thoughts	~~Babies~~
Wedding Gowns	~~Boys~~
~~Washburn Cummings~~	~~Washburn Cummings~~
My Name	~~All My Friends~~
~~My Grandmother~~	~~My Name~~
My Friends	~~My Parents~~
Wordsworth	~~Hospital Rules~~
Christmas	
~~My Parents~~	
Memories (esp. of my wart)	
Washburn Cummings (maybe!)	
My Late Grandmother	
My Parents	
Babies (esp. Sam)	

ABOUT THE AUTHOR

LOIS LOWRY lives in Boston, Massachusetts, where she works as a free-lance journalist, photographer, and writer. Her first book, *A Summer to Die*, won unanimous praise from the critics and received the International Reading Association's Children's Book Award for 1978. It is available from Bantam.

Here are more of the "kid-pleasing" paperbacks that everyone loves.

Bantam Skylark Paperbacks
The Kid-Pleasers

Especially designed for easy reading with large type, wide margins and captivating illustrations, Skylarks are "kid-pleasing" paperbacks featuring the authors, subjects and characters children love.

☐ 15258	BANANA BLITZ Florence Parry Heide	$2.25
☐ 15259	FREAKY FILLINS #1 David Hartley	$1.95
☐ 15250	THE GOOD-GUY CAKE Barbara Dillion	$1.95
☐ 15239	C.L.U.T.Z. Marilyn Wilkes	$1.95
☐ 15237	MUSTARD Charlotte Graeber	$1.95
☐ 15157	ALVIN FERNALD: TV ANCHORMAN Clifford Hicks	$1.95
☐ 15338	ANASTASIA KRUPNIK Lois Lowry	$2.50
☐ 15168	HUGH PINE Janwillen Van de Wetering	$1.95
☐ 15248	CHARLIE AND THE CHOCOLATE FACTORY Roald Dahl	$2.50
☐ 15174	CHARLIE AND THE GREAT GLASS ELEVATOR Roald Dahl	$2.50
☐ 15317	JAMES AND THE GIANT PEACH Roald Dahl	$2.95
☐ 15255	ABEL'S ISLAND William Steig	$2.25
☐ 15194	BIG RED Jim Kjelgaard	$2.50
☐ 15206	IRISH RED: SON OF BIG RED Jim Kjelgaard	$2.25
☐ 01803	JACOB TWO-TWO MEETS THE HOODED FANG Mordecai Richler	$2.95
☐ 15034	TUCK EVERLASTING Natalie Babbitt	$2.25
☐ 15343	THE TWITS Roald Dahl	$2.50

<u>Prices and availability subject to change without notice.</u>

Buy them at your local bookstore or use this handy coupon for ordering:

Bantam Books, Inc., Dept SK, 414 East Golf Road, Des Plaines, Ill. 60016

Please send me the books I have checked above. I am enclosing $_____
(please add $1.25 to cover postage and handling). Send check or money order—
no cash or C.O.D.'s please.

Mr/Mrs/Miss _____

Address _____

City _____ State/Zip _____

SK—8/85
Please allow four to six weeks for delivery. This offer expires 2/86.

JIM KJELGAARD

In these adventure stories, Jim Kjelgaard shows us the special world of animals, the wilderness, and the bonds between men and dogs. *Irish Red* and *Outlaw Red* are stories about two champion Irish setters. *Snow Dog* shows what happens when a half-wild dog crosses paths with a trapper. The cougar-hunting *Lion Hound* and the greyhound story *Desert Dog* take place in our present-day Southwest. And, *Stormy* is an extraordinary story of a boy and his devoted dog. You'll want to read all these exciting books.

☐	15332	A NOSE FOR TROUBLE	$2.25
☐	15121	HAUNT FOX	$1.95
☐	15194	BIG RED	$2.50
☐	15324	DESERT DOG	$2.50
☐	15286	IRISH RED: SON OF BIG RED	$2.50
☐	15247	LION HOUND	$2.50
☐	15339	OUTLAW RED	$2.50
☐	15230	SNOW DOG	$2.25
☐	15215	STORMY	$2.25
☐	15316	WILD TREK	$2.50

Prices and availability subject to change without notice.
Buy them at your local bookstore or use this handy coupon for ordering:

Now you can have your favorite Choose Your Own Adventure® Series in a variety of sizes. Along with the popular pocket size, Bantam has introduced the Choose Your Own Adventure® series in a Skylark edition and also in Hardcover.

Now not only do you get to decide on how you want your adventures to end, you also get to decide on what size you'd like to collect them in.

SKYLARK EDITIONS

☐	15309	The Green Slime #6 S. Saunders	$1.95
☐	15195	Help! You're Shrinking #7 E. Packard	$1.95
☐	15201	Indian Trail #8 R. A. Montgomery	$1.95
☐	15190	Dream Trips #9 E. Packard	$1.95
☐	15191	The Genie In the Bottle #10 J. Razzi	$1.95
☐	15222	The Big Foot Mystery #11 L. Sonberg	$1.95
☐	15223	The Creature From Millers Pond #12 S. Saunders	$1.95
☐	15226	Jungle Safari #13 E. Packard	$1.95
☐	15227	The Search For Champ #14 S. Gilligan	$1.95
☐	15241	Three Wishes #15 S. Gilligan	$1.95
☐	15242	Dragons! #16 J. Razzi	$1.95
☐	15261	Wild Horse Country #17 L. Sonberg	$1.95
☐	15262	Summer Camp #18 J. Gitenstein	$1.95
☐	15270	The Tower of London #19 S. Saunders	$1.95
☐	15271	Trouble In Space #20 J. Woodcock	$1.95
☐	15283	Mona Is Missing #21 S. Gilligan	$1.95
☐	15303	The Evil Wizard #22 A. Packard	$1.95
☐	15305	The Flying Carpet #25	$1.95
☐	15318	The Magic Path #26	$1.95
☐	15331	Ice Cave #27	$1.95

Prices and availability subject to change without notice.

Buy them at your local bookstore or use this handy coupon for ordering:

Bantam Books, Inc., Dept. AVSK, 414 East Golf Road, Des Plaines, Ill. 60016

Please send me the books I have checked above. I am enclosing $_____ (please add $1.25 to cover postage and handling). Send check or money order—no cash or C.O.D.'s please.

Mr/Ms _____

Address _____

City/State _____ Zip _____

AVSK—6/85

Please allow four to six weeks for delivery. This offer expires 12/85.

SPECIAL
MONEY SAVING
OFFER

Now you can have an up-to-date listing of Bantam's hundreds of titles plus take advantage of our unique and exciting bonus book offer. A special offer which gives you the opportunity to purchase a Bantam book for only 50¢. Here's how!

By ordering any five books at the regular price per order, you can also choose any other single book listed (up to a $4.95 value) for just 50¢. Some restrictions do apply, but for further details why not send for Bantam's listing of titles today!

Just send us your name and address plus 50¢ to defray the postage and handling costs.